HEARTS *of* AMISH COUNTRY™

Hearts REUNITED

Rachel J. Good

Annie's®
AnniesFiction.com

Library of Congress-in-Publication Data
Hearts Reunited / by Rachel J. Good
p. cm.
I. Title
                          2017956549

AnniesFiction.com
(800) 282-6643
Hearts of Amish Country™
Series Creator: Shari Lohner
Series Editor: Janice Tate

10 11 12 13 14 | Printed in China | 9 8 7 6 5 4 3 2

Prologue

Rose Ebersol slipped out of the chicken house clutching one of the tamer hens tightly against her chest and headed down the lane to the neighbor's phone shanty. After she closed the shanty door, she set the hen on the floor and scattered some corn on the ground. The chicken ruffled its feathers, squawked, and pecked hard at Rose's shoe before nibbling the corn.

Rose's hands shook as she unfolded the tiny slip of paper she'd secreted in her palm. Was she brave enough to do this? Taking a deep breath to calm her racing pulse, she dialed the number her *Englisch* cousin had given her.

The phone rang. Once . . . twice . . . *Please pick up the phone.* It rang two more times. She didn't have much time. *Daed* would be coming out of the house soon to hook up the horses and drive her to work. The ringing continued.

Her heart sinking, Rose started to hang up the phone when, on the other end, a voice buzzed. Her throat constricted, and she couldn't force out the words she'd rehearsed for days.

"Hello?" the woman said again. "Is anyone there?" Muffled sounds came from the background.

"Wait," Rose said. "Don't hang up, please. My name's Rose Ebersol. My cousin Naomi gave me your number."

"Oh, yes. You must be the girl who wants to be a nurse." The woman sounded as if she were soothing a skittish horse. "We've been expecting your call. You want us to come for you?"

"Y-yes." Rose had to hurry and get out of the shanty. "I work at Zook's Fry Pies. I get off work at nine, but I'm the only cook tonight, so I could sneak out the back door ten minutes early before Daed arrives. There's a little patch of woods nearby where I could hide." Rose pushed the words out in such a rush that they all ran together. Could the woman even understand her? And would she know where Zook's was? Rose had no sense of direction, and her father had never let her drive the buggy. What would she do if they asked her directions?

"I know where that is. We'll have a driver there at precisely 8:53. He won't be able to wait." The woman's voice turned clipped and businesslike. "If you aren't there, we'll assume you changed your mind or weren't able to get away. In that case, feel free to call back with alternate plans."

"Th-thank you," Rose said before the line went dead. What had she done? Could she really defy her parents this way?

"Rose!" her Daed bellowed. "Where are you?"

Oh no! Rose's whole body shook. If Daed discovered her in the phone shanty . . .

She picked up the hen, which clucked and nipped at her hand with its sharp beak. Its claws stabbed her arms through her cotton sleeves. Rose eased the door open, crept to the side of the shanty opposite her house, and set the chicken on the ground, giving it a slight push toward their yard. She chased the fluttering bird across the grass and tackled it where Daed could see her. When she stood, she held the flapping, cackling hen far from her body so she wouldn't be scratched, but it didn't stop the hen from gouging at her hands with its sharp beak.

Daed glowered at her. "How did that hen get out?"

Rose hung her head. "I'm sorry, Daed." *Sorry for everything I've done, for deceiving you, and for what I'm planning to do.*

"We'll discuss this tonight when you get home from work," he snapped as she headed to the chicken coop.

Usually his harsh tone made her tremble. Letting a chicken loose would carry a stiff penalty, but her punishment would be less severe than if she'd been caught coming out of the phone shanty. If all went well, though, she'd never have to face his wrath again.

Rose climbed into the buggy beside Daed, her heart pounding so hard her chest ached. She hoped he couldn't hear it thundering. She glanced over her shoulder for one last glimpse of the farmhouse and blinked back the tears threatening to fall.

The short trip to Zook's seemed to stretch on and on until Rose was so tense she could barely sit still. She wriggled in her seat, willing the horse to trot faster, willing this ride to end.

Daed frowned. "Stop all that *rutsching.*"

Rose clutched fistfuls of her skirt to calm her jittering and forced her upper body into stillness, but her legs quivered beneath her full skirt. When the horse stopped in front of Zook's, Rose released a pent-up breath. With misty eyes, she imprinted her father's profile in her memory. He might be strict, or even harsh, but he loved her and cared for their family. She wished she could have said goodbye to her sister and *Mamm.* It was hard to believe she might never see them again.

Daed flicked a hand toward the building. "Get on with you so you're not late."

With a lump of sorrow blocking her throat, Rose could barely manage to say, "Yes Daed," before she left the buggy and headed into the shop. The heavy odor of frying oil mingling with the sweet scent of melting icing made Rose's eyes sting. Only three hours to go before she left here forever. After tonight, she'd never smell this again. Never see Martha. Never see her friends and family.

When she'd closed the door behind her, she pressed her face against the latticed window and stared out into the growing dusk until Daed's buggy disappeared in the distance. She rubbed her eyes to clear them before she turned. Her best friend, Martha, already stood behind the counter, a frown wrinkling her brow.

"Are you all right?" she whispered as Rose walked past her to the kitchen.

"I'm fine," Rose said, her voice shaky.

Martha raised an eyebrow. She was well aware of Rose's struggles at home. "Trouble with your Daed again?" She kept her voice low so the customers waiting at the counter couldn't hear.

Rose disliked lying to her friend, but she had to say something. "He's upset about a hen getting loose." *A small worry compared with the one I am about to cause.* "I'd better get back there and relieve Jonas."

She'd have to avoid Martha tonight. Her friend was much too perceptive. If they spent any time together, Rose might be tempted to spill her plans. If she did, Martha would try to talk her out of leaving.

Jonas greeted Rose with a smile. "I'll take this last batch of lemon pies out of the fryer before I go, but we're low on most of the pies—strawberry, blueberry, peach—as well as cherry and apple. The dough's already mixed."

Rose washed her hands at the small sink and dried them well. She fumbled as she picked up the rolling pin. It slid off the counter and crashed onto the floor, making Jonas jump.

He turned to stare at her. "You all right?" When she nodded, he lifted the basket filled with crispy pies, letting the hot oil drip back into the fryer. He shook the basket a few times before flipping the steaming pies onto the rack to drain.

Rose washed and dried the rolling pin, then grabbed a ball of dough. Rolling the dough flat helped calm her shaky hands, but nothing could calm her roiling stomach.

Jonas drizzled icing on top and picked up the rack. "I'll take these out to Martha."

Once again Rose only nodded. A hurt look crossed his face, making her feel guilty. Ordinarily she enjoyed talking to Jonas, but tonight she didn't trust herself to speak. She bent her head and pretended to focus on cutting the six-inch circles. Jonas sighed and went out to the counter where he chatted with Martha for a few minutes before leaving. Rose was grateful to have the small kitchen area to herself for the next three hours. Friday nights were so busy, Martha wouldn't have time to pop in to talk. And by the time Martha finished cleaning the counters and the small seating area, Rose would be long gone.

For the next few hours, Rose rolled dough, cut circles, fed them and the pie fillings into the press, and turned the crank to seal and crimp the edges. As one batch went into the fryer, she started another. She iced the hot pies and, with a pasted-on smile, handed the trays out to Martha. Every step mechanical, she kept her mind blank, but each time she looked at the clock, the hands had barely inched along. About ten minutes before she planned to leave, she began cleaning the kitchen and left Martha a note. She'd give her friend one more batch. When the pies finished frying, Rose glanced up at the clock. Only three minutes to get to the meeting spot. She drizzled on icing and shoved the tray in Martha's direction. With less than a minute to go, she flicked the fryer knobs, flung the dish towel, and raced out the door. If she didn't make it by 8:53, she'd never have the courage to call again.

1

Jonathan Fisher rubbed his forehead, trying to ease his headache before he knocked at his brother's front door. With a loud creak, the door opened to reveal Jonathan's four-year-old daughter, Hannah. When she gazed up at him, her blue eyes and blonde hair reminded him so much of his wife, it hurt to look at her.

"Daed!" she exclaimed, launching herself at his knees.

Every muscle ached, but Jonathan hid his grimace as he bent and scooped her into his arms. "Ready to go?"

His sister-in-law, Martha, came up behind Hannah, cradling baby Amos. She stood at an angle to him, hiding her scarred right cheek and neck, and Jonathan averted his eyes. He avoided looking directly at that side of her face, not only because she was self-conscious about it but also because seeing her skin grafts brought up a miserable time in his life. Memories he only wanted to forget. Memories of Rose, the first girl he'd ever loved, the girl who'd broken his heart, the girl responsible for those scars.

Martha studied him. "You look terrible. Were you up all night?" Though she often spoke bluntly, she had a sweet, caring nature.

"Just about. The calf was finally born about two a.m. It was a rough delivery."

"And you had to get up at four this morning to milk the cows," she said, her eyes full of sympathy. "Why don't you leave the children here again tonight so you can get some rest?"

"Then you won't get any sleep."

Martha bent her head and cooed at Amos. "I don't mind missing sleep for this precious little one." When she lifted her head, her hazel eyes glistened with tears. "I need someone to fill these empty arms. Until God blesses us with children, I get great joy in mothering yours."

The word *mother* pierced Jonathan. He pinched his lips together to hold back the waves of grief threatening to engulf him, and he hugged his daughter closer. When he spoke, his voice came out husky. "I appreciate all you've done for my little ones." He couldn't have managed without her and his brother David. The two of them had helped to care for the children every day for the past eight months, since the day his wife, Esther, died giving birth to Amos.

"It's been my pleasure."

Martha's voice quavered, and Jonathan's heart ached for her. She and his brother David were heartbroken over their inability to have children. Perhaps God had kept them waiting because He knew they'd be needed to assist his family. Jonathan didn't want to overburden them, though. Martha had kept all three children last night in addition to watching them during the day while he worked.

Getting up at four to milk cows and then planting and tending his organic vegetables before the afternoon milking meant he had no opportunity to watch the children during the day. Then he got little sleep whenever Amos was fussy from teething or Hannah woke in the middle of the night, whimpering, missing her Mamm. Libby, at age two, was the best sleeper, but even she had restless nights. And this spring, the birth of calves had meant late nights in the barn.

He looked around for his younger daughter. Usually she toddled out to meet him when he arrived. "Where's Libby?" he asked.

Hannah lifted her head from his shoulder. "Sleeping."

"Libby's already down for the night," Martha said. "All the more reason to let the children stay here. No point in waking her to take her home to bed."

At the thought of the long, dark night alone in his empty house, Jonathan's spirits plummeted. But he didn't want to disturb his daughter's sleep for his own selfish needs. Whenever he didn't have the children's cries to respond to at night, he slept fitfully, restlessly, if he even closed his eyes at all. When he did, sadness washed over him, pressing down on his chest, choking him, and that sorrow carried over into his dreams.

Martha interrupted his thoughts. "You haven't eaten yet, have you?"

If he said he hadn't, she'd insist on feeding him, but he couldn't lie. "Not yet, but I'll fix something when I get home."

"I figured you'd forget to eat." She lifted Amos over her shoulder and patted his back. "I have a pot of chicken corn soup simmering on the stove."

She always tempted him with his favorite foods. He hadn't had much of an appetite these past few months and often skipped meals, so Martha considered it her duty to see that he ate.

"You don't have to feed me," Jonathan said. "You've done enough already with caring for the children."

Martha ignored his protest and beckoned for him to follow her to the kitchen. "*Cum esse.*"

Turning down her invitation to come and eat would hurt her feelings, so Jonathan trailed her to the kitchen. One part of him wanted to refuse, but onions perfumed the air and the warm chicken broth bubbling on the stove made his mouth water. He sat Hannah on the floor and settled into his usual place at the table. Hannah slid onto the bench beside him and leaned her head against his arm, easing some of his loneliness.

Martha put Amos on the spotless linoleum, and he crawled over to the table. Gripping the edge of the wooden bench, he pulled himself to his feet beside Jonathan. A lump in his throat, Jonathan laid a hand on his son's soft blond bangs. His heart swelled with love whenever he looked at his tiny son, but his joy was bittersweet. He was grateful for the gift of his son, although that gift had come at a great price.

Why was love so often accompanied by loss? He'd married Esther after he lost Rose. He'd pushed Rose out of his mind and concentrated on being a good husband. He and Esther had grown closer over their years together, and her death left a huge, aching gap.

He forced a smile as Martha set a bowl brimming with corn, celery, noodles, and chunks of chicken in front of him, along with a plate of sliced homemade bread. Closing his eyes and bowing his head, Jonathan said the Lord's Prayer silently before dipping a spoon into the fragrant, steaming broth. The warmth sliding down his throat to his stomach comforted him, but the heat couldn't melt the iciness surrounding his heart.

When he scraped the last bits from his bowl, Martha scurried over. "Let me get you another bowlful."

Jonathan shook his head and pushed back the bench. "*Danke*, the soup was delicious and filling, but I need to get home."

Much as he wished he could stay in this warm kitchen and avoid going back to his empty house, they all needed their sleep. They'd rise before dawn for milking goats or cows, so going to bed early was an ingrained habit. He wished he could help Martha wash his dishes and redd up the kitchen to prevent her from staying up later than usual. Although he did dishes at home, she would be offended if he offered to help.

"I'm sorry for making extra work," he said, swinging Amos into his arms and reaching out a hand to Hannah, who was wriggling off the bench. When her small warm hand clasped his, his heart overflowed with thankfulness.

"*Ach*, it's no trouble." Martha placed the bowl in the sink. "I'm happy to do it."

"Danke for everything," he said, turning to go. "I'll just head out to the barn to tell David good night."

Martha shooed him with her hand. "Get on with you. I'll tell David you were here. Go home and get some sleep." She reached for Amos. "I'll get this little angel ready for bed. The water's already on, and his bottle's heating."

Reluctantly, Jonathan surrendered his son to Martha's waiting arms, leaving his own empty. He'd been planning to take Amos home, but if it was time for his son's bottle, he shouldn't disrupt the feeding schedule. Martha had established a routine for Amos during the dark days after Esther's passing, when Jonathan's mind was so fogged he couldn't make any decisions. They'd kept to it ever since. Jonathan wanted to beg her to forget the schedule for one night, to let him hold Amos longer, but Martha was already bustling off to the stove for the bottle.

"Come along, Hannah," she called over her shoulder. "Time for you to get ready for bed."

"I want to stay with Daed!" Hannah wailed, clinging to his knees.

Jonathan picked up his daughter. "I'll take her home with me."

Martha's forehead wrinkled in concern. "I don't think—"

"She'll be fine," Jonathan assured her. "Likely she'll fall asleep on the way home, and I can just tuck her into bed."

"But what about your sleep? It doesn't make sense for both of us to lose sleep."

No, it didn't, but with Hannah's arms wound around his neck and her eyes pleading with him, Jonathan couldn't bear to let her go. "We'll be all right."

Martha shook her head, but she held her peace. She tested the milk on her forearm and then held the bottle to Amos's lips. His son drank greedily.

After another Danke for all Martha had done, Jonathan brushed Amos's bangs off his forehead and ran a finger along his cheek. Leaving Amos and Libby behind tore Jonathan apart inside. He turned before Martha could see the wistfulness in his eyes, and wrapping his arms tightly around Hannah, he strode to the back door.

Although Martha had offered to pass along a message to David, Jonathan wanted to at least say hello to his brother, so he headed outside and across the backyard. When he opened the barn door, the faint scent of bleach wafted out. Being especially careful with Hannah in his arms, Jonathan picked his way along the wet and slippery cement that had already been hosed down. David was cleaning and soaking the black rubber hoses from his milking equipment, a daily chore to meet the strict safety standards they kept at their dairies.

"Hey, Jonathan." David always saved an extra-special smile for Hannah. "Did you tell your Daed you fed the cows and helped empty the milk today?"

Hannah smiled back but buried her head against Jonathan's neck when she shook her head.

Jonathan patted her back. "You're becoming a big helper, Hannah." Then he turned to his brother. "Is that cow any better?"

David shook his head. "The vet was here and gave her some antibiotics. Hope that'll help. Have to keep her isolated until her milk tests all right again." He brushed the parts before rinsing them. "Your delivery go well last night?"

"It was a rough one, but the calf's doing fine."

David held a hose under running water. "Good, good. Births are always a miracle."

Yes, they were, but sometimes . . . Jonathan turned his head away and pretended to inspect the cow in the nearest stall so his brother couldn't see his pain.

"I'm sorry," David said. "I should have thought . . ."

"It's all right." Blinking back the moisture in his eyes, Jonathan turned to face his brother. "I know what you meant." He winced at the pity in his brother's eyes. One of the hardest parts of dealing with a death, besides the depth of grief, was handling the pitying looks.

"*Jah*, well . . ." David shuffled his feet and concentrated on cleaning the next hose. "I hope Martha fed you."

Jonathan was grateful for the change of subject. "She did. The chicken corn soup was delicious. You have a good wife in Martha. I hope you appreciate her."

"I do." David gazed off into the distance. "I wish the fire hadn't happened for Martha's sake, but if it hadn't, we never would have started courting." He reached out a hand and squeezed Jonathan's shoulder. "Good often comes out of tragedy."

Jonathan nodded and shifted Hannah in his arms. He'd never seen the good come out of Rose's dating David, of her leaving, or of his most recent heartbreak—Esther's death. "Well, I'd better get Hannah home. It's late."

"Good idea." David set down the last hose and walked them out to the wagon. "Drive safely," he said as he always did.

Jonathan nodded, his throat too tight to answer.

After they climbed into the wagon, Hannah snuggled against him. Jonathan switched the reins to one hand so he could hold her close with his other arm. Her nearness comforted him, and he hoped he eased some of her sadness.

"Daed?" His daughter's soft voice was barely audible over the horse's clomping hooves and the rattle of the wagon wheels.

"Yes, Hannah?"

Her lower lip quivered. "When's Mamm coming back?"

Jonathan's hand tightened on the reins, and he squeezed his eyes shut. When he opened them again, the road appeared slightly blurred. "She won't be coming back. She's in heaven now."

"Not ever?" Hannah's words held a note of disbelief. "*Daadi* visited *Onkel* Ezra, but he came back. *Aenti* Dorcas was gone a long, long time, but she came home yesterday."

They'd been over this several times since the funeral, but Hannah persisted in believing her Mamm would return. Martha's sister Dorcas had just returned from Mexico, where she'd gone for cancer treatments, and that must have prompted this discussion.

Jonathan swallowed hard. "Yes, they came back. But when you go to heaven, you stay there forever."

"Forever and ever?" Tears trickled down Hannah's cheeks.

Jonathan hugged her more tightly to his side, wishing he could wipe away her tears and comfort her. But he had no remedy for her grief. "Someday you'll see her in heaven."

"I don't want to wait."

"I know, but God has other plans for us here." If only he knew what those were, and why God had taken Esther so young, leaving behind three motherless children.

2

Rose gripped the metal pole with one hand and the handle of her wheeled suitcase with the other as the train squealed to a stop. Her stop. The doors slid open, and passengers shoved and elbowed each other to be the first to exit. Her stomach in knots, Rose smoothed down the plain dress she'd donned for the trip, but the now-unfamiliar clothes only increased her anxiety. What if she stayed on the train and let it carry her back to the city, back to the place she belonged? Her real home.

Boarding passengers swarmed into the crowded car, yet fear kept her glued to the cracked leather seat. She longed to stay on this train and head back to New York.

A loud muffled voice in the station announced the train was departing. As the train shuddered and the doors slid closed, Rose gathered her courage, leaped from the seat, and hurried to the door, dragging her suitcase. A man slid a hand into the crack of the almost-shut door, and it opened. She shot him a grateful look and, heart pounding, exited onto the bustling platform of the station.

She'd arrived. The first leg of her journey was complete, but the most difficult part was about to begin. Late-spring sunshine warmed her back as she tugged her suitcase toward the black wrought iron railings and concrete steps leading to the outside world, the world she dreaded entering, the world she'd fled from seven years ago.

Her apprehension intensified as she mounted the stairs, her suitcase bumping along behind. When she reached the top, she stopped to catch her breath and muster her courage. Her suitcase wheels squeaked on the linoleum as she crossed the high-ceilinged waiting room, pushed open the heavy exterior doors, and reemerged in the sunlight.

She'd dawdled so long that all the waiting taxis had departed with passengers; she'd have to call a cab company. As she reached into her purse for her glasses and cell phone, a passing buggy slowed, and the driver stared at her. Though some of the Amish now had cell phones, Rose couldn't rid herself of the old guilty feelings of breaking rules, so she tucked her phone into the folds of her skirt until he passed.

But rather than trotting by, the man slowed his horse to a crawl. His face was blurry, and Rose wished she had on her glasses so she could see who it was. Was he slowing because he had business at the station, or because he recognized her? She'd hoped to get to her parents' house without seeing anyone she knew.

The wagon stopped, and the man called out. "Do you need help?"

Though his voice had grown deeper, Rose would have recognized it anywhere. She sucked in a deep breath to calm her jumpy nerves and racing pulse.

The voice belonged to Jonathan Fisher. The one person she most wanted to avoid.

After being up all night with Hannah, Jonathan had been yawning and rubbing his eyes as he drove past the station to deliver his organic vegetables to the Farm to Table Restaurant. His vision might have been clouded, but his heart thudded faster as a woman came out the door. He shook his head. It couldn't be Rose Ebersol. He scrubbed at his sleep-bleary eyes again with his fists, but the mirage persisted.

The woman had Rose's sweet smile, although her posture seemed wary, almost defensive, and she was dressed in plain clothes. Definitely not Rose. Rose Ebersol had left for the Englisch world. Still, this woman appeared confused and uncertain. She must have come to visit relatives. He should try to help her find her way, or perhaps she needed a ride.

Hopping out of the wagon, he headed toward her, although she hadn't responded to his question. Maybe she hadn't heard him with all the noise and traffic. As he approached, he asked again, "Can I help—?" His voice faltered. He'd been wrong.

It most definitely was Rose.

"Jonathan?" Her cheeks flushed, she fumbled with something in her hand, trying to hide it in the folds of her dress.

A cell phone.

"Were you planning to call someone?" He gestured toward the phone, and her blush deepened.

"I, um, planned to call a cab."

"Where are you headed?"

Rose hesitated a moment. "My parents' house."

"Really?" Jonathan tried not to show his surprise.

Rose ducked her head. "Yes." She sounded uncertain of her answer. Or perhaps she was unsure of her welcome.

"But I thought . . ." Jonathan didn't want to repeat gossip.

"That Daed refuses to see me?" Rose finished his sentence with a trace of hurt and bitterness.

Jonathan nodded. Everyone in the community knew of Eli Ebersol's unbending stance toward his daughter. He'd forbidden his wife and daughter to communicate with Rose. So why was she headed home?

Rose must have read the question in his eyes. "You're wondering what I'm doing here?" She didn't wait for his response but hurried on. "AnaMary learned where I worked from our cousin, Naomi. She sent a letter to me at the hospital, begging me to come. Daed's refusing to follow the doctor's orders. She wants me to help care for him. I have no idea what she expects me to do. I told her Daed won't listen to me, and my presence might upset him, even worsen his heart condition . . ."

After her words trailed off, Jonathan wanted to reassure her, but knowing her Daed's fury, he could offer little comfort. Still, he had to say something. "Perhaps when he sees you again, he'll—"

"He'll what? Realize how furious he is at me and have another heart attack?"

"No no. I was going to say he'd be happy you're back. Especially when he sees you're ready to join the church." Jonathan waved a hand toward her dress.

"Oh, no." Dismay in her eyes, Rose pressed a knuckle against her lips. "I didn't mean to mislead people. I only put on plain clothes so I wouldn't upset him."

Although it shouldn't have mattered so much to him, Jonathan couldn't help but be disappointed in her answer. "So you have no intention of joining the church?"

Tears filled Rose's eyes. "I still have my faith, but I could never give up nursing. It's my life."

"I see." As soon as the words were out of his mouth, Jonathan cringed inside. His tone sounded judgmental rather than understanding. He hadn't meant to censure her, but the heaviness in his soul had spilled out into his words. He didn't agree with her choice, but that was between her and God.

"Yes, well, I don't mean to keep you." Rose's voice quavered, indicating he'd hurt her.

"I'm sorry. I didn't mean to sound so critical. It's just that—" *I care about you.* Jonathan froze in place. Where had that thought come from? Of course, he meant he cared about her welfare, like he did about his Daed's, his brother's, and Martha's. That was what he meant, right?

Jonathan shook his head to banish thoughts that were whispering otherwise. Flicking his gaze in her direction, he saw she was waiting for him to finish his sentence. "It's just, um, we all care about you and want to see you back in the church."

Her face fell a little, but then she smiled one of her brilliant smiles. The one that made his insides do cartwheels. He stopped himself from grinning and confined himself to a half smile. He shouldn't be spending so much time with her here in public. He was a widower still in mourning, and she was—despite her clothing—an *Englischer* now.

Rose shuffled her feet and pulled her suitcase closer. "I'd better let you get on with whatever you were doing."

"I have vegetables to deliver to a restaurant nearby. I need to get them there before the chef starts preparing recipes for the evening meals. And then I have to get back home to milk the cows." He was babbling.

"I won't keep you then."

He should let her go and hurry to his delivery, but he couldn't leave her stranded. "Have you already called a taxi?"

Rose shook her head. "But I will."

"If you don't mind waiting while I drop off the crates, I'd be happy to take you home." As soon as he said it, Jonathan regretted his invitation. Riding with Rose in the wagon would stir up memories best left forgotten.

"Danke for your kind offer, but I couldn't trouble you. You have work to do."

What was the matter with him? First he wished he hadn't offered, but now that she'd declined, his spirits had plunged. "It's no problem. I go right past your farm."

Rose hesitated. The last thing she wanted to do was get in the wagon with him, but the old feelings flooding through her made her reluctant to let him leave. The minute she'd recognized his voice, her pulse had started zinging, and being near him . . . Rose reined in her runaway thoughts.

He was only being neighborly; he wouldn't understand if she declined. He had no idea he was the main reason she'd fled to New York. Keeping him waiting while she dithered might make him late for his delivery.

"If you're sure it's no bother," she said, her words breathy, "I'd appreciate a ride."

His tight smile widened into a genuine grin, then wavered, to be replaced by a sober expression. Rose ducked her head to hide her disappointment. What had she expected? He was a married man.

She bent to grab the handle of her suitcase at the same time he leaned over and reached for it. Their hands brushed and tingling shot up Rose's arm. Jonathan yanked his hand back.

"Let me get your bag," he said.

Rose almost retorted she could do it herself. She was used to taking care of her own needs in New York, but it would be rude to reject his polite offer. She let go of the handle and backed up. "Danke," she said.

He stood stiffly and waited until she'd moved a safe distance away. Then he took the handle and motioned to his wagon. Rose followed him and climbed in while he moved some of his crates to make room for her suitcase.

They rode in silence for a few minutes while Jonathan negotiated the busy intersection and entered the flow of traffic. Rose held her breath as he eased to the side of the road to let cars zip by. It had been so long since she'd been this exposed while traveling. She'd flinched at the speed and heaviness of traffic in New York and panicked her first few months of taking the subway, but now she was used to being in enclosed spaces while she traveled. Riding in the wagon made her feel vulnerable, almost as vulnerable as sitting beside Jonathan.

Her constricted breathing wasn't only from the nearness of traffic. Rose averted her eyes from the man beside her, avoiding the temptation to study how his chest and shoulders had broadened and how his face had developed strong, masculine lines. He looked even more handsome with a beard than he had as a clean-shaven teen. But his beard, which made him look more mature and attractive, showed he belonged to another woman. She had no right to assess his looks or react to him this way.

Rose grasped for a topic of conversation to break the awkward silence. Taking a deep breath, she asked, "So how's your family? Do you have children?"

Sadness flickered in Jonathan's eyes for a moment, but he answered, "Yes, three of them. Hannah's four and a big help in the house and barn already. Libby's two, and Amos is"—his Adam's apple bobbed up and down—"eight months."

Her insides twisted. He and Esther had been married for six years now. Of course they'd have children. He hadn't mentioned Esther. News about his wife would cut her deeply, but it would be impolite not to ask after her. Rose forced herself to say, "And how is—"

Jonathan interrupted her question by pulling the wagon to the curb. "I'll try not to take too long." He jumped down, hurried to the back of the wagon, and hefted two heavy crates. His muscles rippled under his shirt as he strode to the restaurant service entrance with the slatted wooden boxes.

He emerged smiling and caught her eye, stealing Rose's breath and leaving her dizzy. She struggled to tear her gaze away and stare at her hands, which she'd clasped tightly in her lap, but she couldn't resist watching him unload the rest of the crates.

After he had emptied the wagon, he climbed in beside her and clucked to the horse. "Sorry to keep you waiting."

"I didn't mind." *Not at all.* She'd enjoyed the view. Her cheeks heated, and she blurted out, "So you're selling vegetables now?"

Jonathan nodded but kept his gaze on the road. For a moment she thought he might not answer. "About four years ago, we started an organic farm. A lot of restaurants in the area want to serve organic foods, so I worked on growing specialty vegetables. It's worked out well."

"You're not dairy farming anymore?" Rose sucked in a breath and gripped the wagon seat as a car roared past.

Jonathan slowed to make a turn. "I do that too. And now that Daed's so frail, David—" He glanced sideways at her as if to assess her reaction, but when she kept her expression neutral, he continued, "Well, he helps Daed on the farm too."

Rose tamped down the tension swirling inside at the mention of David's name. She and David had been good friends, but when everyone else in their youth group paired up, so had the two of them. No one had ever known Rose's secret, not even David. She'd been in love with David's older brother. The man sitting beside her. The man who was now married to someone else.

3

After Jonathan dropped her off at her parents' house, Rose stood on the doorstep, her hand poised to knock, but she waited until he'd driven off. If Daed ordered her out into the street, she didn't want Jonathan to witness her humiliation. And now that she was here, she had cold feet. She'd fled her Daed's strict rules to follow her dreams. And if she were honest, to escape a broken heart. If it hadn't been for her sister AnaMary's pleading letter, she never would have returned.

Bowing her head, she prayed for strength to face whatever lay ahead. Then, taking a deep breath, she tapped at the door. Inside someone shuffled across the floor, and the door opened.

Mamm stood in the doorway, her face more wrinkled and her back more bowed. She peered at Rose, a puzzled expression on her face. Then her eyes widened, and her mouth opened in an *O*.

"Rose?" Mamm's face bloomed into a smile. "You're back." She opened her arms wide but glanced over her shoulder to the closed bedroom door. Her joyful expression shriveled into lines of tension, and her arms dropped to her sides. "Your Daed . . ." She gestured helplessly. "I don't think . . ."

AnaMary rushed from the kitchen. "You came!" she said in an excited whisper. "I didn't know if you would."

Mamm planted her hands on her hips. "You asked your sister to come home?" Her voice low but scolding, she said, "You disobeyed your Daed."

"We need help, Mamm." AnaMary waved an impatient hand.

"Rose is a nurse. She'll know what to do."

Their Mamm frowned. "That may be, but you should not have gone against your Daed's wishes." Her voice shook. "He's going to be furious."

And her mother would bear the blame. Rose had to find a way to shield Mamm from Daed's wrath. "I'll explain I came of my own accord, and you weren't expecting me."

"Right," AnaMary said. "And we didn't even want to let you in. Look how we've kept you on the porch all this time."

Rose picked up her sister's cue and pushed on the door, then stepped over the threshold. "And I forced my way in."

AnaMary winked at her. "We tried to resist"—she shoved on the door as if to keep Rose out—"but you overpowered me."

Mamm's hands remained on her hips, and although the corners of her lips lifted slightly, her voice was stern. "You will not lie to your father."

"Of course not," AnaMary said, but her tone was flippant. "We were only teasing."

When had her younger sister become so defiant? As a child AnaMary had been docile and compliant. Judging by the rebellious gleam in her eyes, she must be a handful during *Rumschpringe.*

Like you, Rose's conscience nagged. She hoped her example wouldn't cause her sister to leave the community. She'd take AnaMary aside and explain the pain and loneliness accompanying that decision.

Mamm wrung her hands. "I shouldn't have let you in. Your Daed's napping now, but when he wakes, he'll be livid."

Rose reached for the doorknob. She didn't want to rile Daed or cause friction between her parents.

But AnaMary grasped her arm. "No, you can't go. Not without trying to convince Daed to follow the doctor's orders." She ended on a shrill note.

"Hush," Mamm warned, but it was too late.

"Miriam?" Daed barked from the bedroom.

Mamm's face pinched into a worried frown. Motioning for Rose to leave, she scurried to the bedroom door. "Yes, Eli?" Her voice quavered. "Are you ready for your dinner?"

"Who is AnaMary talking to?"

Mamm glanced over her shoulder, her face ashen and eyes desperate. Still clutching Rose's arm, AnaMary marched to the bedroom doorway, dragging Rose along with her.

Charging into the room, she said, "I was talking to your nurse." She gestured toward Rose. "She's here to be sure you do what Dr. Hess said."

Daed squinted at Rose. Then recognition dawned in his eyes, and his face darkened. "You do not belong here!" he thundered. "How dare you enter this house after what you've done?"

Rose shrank back from the force of his rage. "I'm sorry, Daed." She was not sorry for leaving, but she regretted the hurt she'd caused her family.

His face still twisted with rage, he studied her. "Have you come back to join the church?"

Wearing plain clothes had been a mistake. First Jonathan and now Daed had misunderstood her intentions. She hadn't wanted to offend her family by flaunting her Englisch clothes. Instead, she'd given them a false impression.

Her throat dry, Rose forced herself to answer honestly, although she was risking even greater fury. "No, Daed. I came back to help nurse you."

He turned to Mamm. "You never should have let her in. Get her out of here now!" His screaming drowned out Mamm's pleading apologies. "And you," he shouted, pointing a finger at Rose, "you've torn apart this household by your rebelliousness!"

Rose pinned him with a stare. "I'm going, but your temper is one of the main reasons I left. I hope you don't drive AnaMary away too."

Fear froze her tongue as Daed puffed up like a rattler about to strike. His eyes narrowed. "Blaming me does not excuse your guilt." His voice low and menacing, he added, "Unless you bend your knee and join the church, you are not welcome in this house ever again."

Rose whirled and headed for the door. She regretted her disrespect and sharp words, but her throat was so tight, she couldn't speak or apologize.

AnaMary followed her. "I'm so sorry," she whispered, tears filming her eyes. "I only wanted to bring the family together. And to help Daed recover. I should have known this would happen. I thought . . ."

Rose touched her arm. "Don't blame yourself."

"Shut that door, AnaMary," Daed ordered. "Now!"

Sympathy in her eyes, AnaMary closed the front door, leaving Rose alone on the porch with her suitcase. If only Rose had followed her instincts and remained on the train, she'd be partway back to New York by now. Back where she belonged.

Spending time with Rose had put Jonathan behind schedule, so he was a bit late starting the milking. When he arrived at Martha's that evening, she greeted him at the door.

"Cum esse," she invited, as she always did. "I've kept some meat loaf and twice-baked potatoes warming in the oven for you."

He had little desire to eat tonight but, too tired to protest, he followed her to the kitchen. He'd been on an emotional roller coaster ever since he'd seen Rose. He fought back all the old memories that surfaced by reminding himself of Esther and the bond they'd shared. Yet whenever his hands were busy and his mind was free to roam, he found himself daydreaming about Rose. Not the Englisch one he'd seen today, but the one he'd fallen in love with almost a decade ago.

Fourteen-year-old Rose in her plain dress and *Kapp* had stolen his heart. But she was much too young. During his *Rumschpringe*, he'd kept his distance from girls while his friends paired off. He hid his feelings for Rose, determined to wait until she was old enough to court. Instead, she and his younger brother, David, who was in Rose's buddy bunch, became inseparable. Best friends from childhood, they did everything together. Knowing he had no chance with Rose, Jonathan turned to Esther Zook, a kind girl whom other boys had passed by. She'd been a good wife, and he'd been devoted to her, but he'd never forgotten his first love.

Jonathan washed up and slumped at the table, struggling to erase the memories. He shouldn't be thinking about another woman, especially not one who was Englisch. Rose had made it clear today she had no intention of returning to the Amish.

Martha plunked a plate in front of him. The juice oozing from the meat loaf spiced the air with onion, pepper, tomato, and mustard, whetting his appetite. He'd prayed and forked the first bite into his mouth when it dawned on him that the house was quiet. He'd been so preoccupied with thoughts of Rose, he hadn't noticed Hannah and Libby hadn't rushed out to greet him.

Glancing around the room, he asked, "Where are the girls and Amos?"

Martha turned her back and busied herself with washing dishes. "They went to bed a little early tonight."

"But I didn't get to spend time with them." He cherished that brief time every evening. Missing them started an ache deep within, one that left a large empty hole inside.

"Jah, *vell*, David and I, we have an important matter to discuss with you. I thought it best if the little ones didn't overhear."

The flaky bite of cheesy potato he'd put in his mouth lost its tang. He swallowed the tasteless lump. He hoped her ominous tone didn't mean she and David wouldn't be able to care for the children anymore. He had no one else to ask.

He put a few more bites in his mouth and chewed mechanically. If only he could push his plate away with food still on it, but wasting food was not the Amish way. His stomach rebelled, but he lifted bite after flavorless bite to his mouth until the plate was empty.

Martha whisked the plate away and hurried it over to the sink. "Why don't you sit in the living room while I call David?"

Although he was the older brother, Martha and David had taken over directing his life, and he'd been too tired and overwhelmed to assert himself. As much as he appreciated all they'd done for him, he needed to take control of his life again. He'd insist on seeing the children before he went home from now on and ask Martha not to put them to bed before he arrived.

The back door slammed, and a few minutes later, David entered the room, followed by Martha. At the grave expression on his brother's face and the tension lines around Martha's eyes and mouth, Jonathan's anxiety rose. After a brief greeting, David settled onto the couch, and Martha sat beside him, her back rigid, wringing her hands in her lap. They had news he didn't want to hear.

David cleared his throat, but Martha spoke first: "We're worried about the children."

"Why? Are they ill?" Maybe that's why they were in bed so early. Jonathan jumped up from the couch. "What's wrong?"

David held up a calming hand before Jonathan could charge up the stairs to check on them. "Nothing's wrong with them, at least not

health-wise, but we've been concerned about them for a while now."
He turned to Martha, nodding to indicate that she should pick up
the conversation.

Jonathan sank onto the edge of the chair. The children had all
seemed fine yesterday. He hadn't seen Libby, but . . .

Martha pinched her lips together for a moment. "This isn't an easy
thing to say, but David and I have been talking. We're worried about the
children. It's not good for them to bounce from house to house. They
sleep at your place one night and here another. That's hard on them."

Jonathan agreed. He shouldn't burden Martha and David with
them at night.

When he didn't respond, Martha continued, "David and I think
they'd be better off staying here full time."

It took a moment for her suggestion to sink in. Surely, he'd
misheard. She couldn't be proposing to take his children away. Before
he could protest, she swept on.

"They need stability, a consistent place to live, someone to teach
them to do chores."

"I can do that," Jonathan said.

Martha raised one eyebrow. "You'll teach Hannah and Libby to
cook, do dishes, mop floors, and wash laundry?"

He clasped his hands in his lap. Yes, he struggled with those jobs.
The house never looked as clean and well kept as it had when Esther
was alive, unless Martha or one of Esther's sisters stopped by to do
laundry and redd up. Even if he could teach the girls, when would he
have the time when he worked straight through from predawn to early
evening six days a week?

"And someone needs to do their hair in the morning."

Jonathan's face heated. He'd tried to pull Hannah's hair back into
a bob that morning, but it was the messiest bun he'd ever seen.

As soon as they'd walked into the house, Martha had carried Hannah to the kitchen table, undone the knotted mess, and rolled the hair tightly on each side of her head. With swift fingers and practiced movements, she had turned Hannah's long hair into a tight, neat ball at her nape. Libby's hair was too short and fine to put into a bob, so Martha braided her hair into two short pigtails on either side of her head. The only time he'd tried that, Libby's blonde pigtails had frizzed out all over like dandelion fuzz.

"They need a consistent morning routine. All the hurrying to get here so early in the morning interrupts their sleep. If they were here, they could sleep past dawn, then start their day with grooming, chores, and breakfast all in one place."

Martha was right. Rushing around in the morning, sometimes eating a quick breakfast at home, other times eating here, was hard on the girls. And they often didn't have time for chores or proper grooming before he put them in the wagon to head to David's house. Their evening schedule was even more hectic. They never knew whether they'd sleep here or at home.

As the silence stretched between them, the tension in Martha's face relaxed. She must have known she'd made her point.

But Jonathan couldn't give up that easily. Not when it came to his children. "Maybe I could give up the vegetables so I'd be free during the day."

David leaned forward, his eyes filled with concern. "You haven't paid off the milking equipment yet, have you?"

Jonathan met his brother's gaze. "Not yet."

"I thought you were using the vegetable money to pay off your loans."

"I am. But I've been paying double payments most months. I could still meet the monthly payments without it." *If I take money out of the emergency fund I set aside for doctor bills, vet visits, and . . .*

"You're sure?" David pinned him with a gaze.

"Well, it'd be tight." *Too tight.*

Martha had only gotten started, though. "Leaving the children here would make things much easier for you. You wouldn't have to worry when you work late, you'd get good sleep at night, you'd . . ."

Her voice trailed off when Jonathan frowned. "I know you'd miss them, but you're welcome here anytime. And really, it wouldn't be much different than it is now."

Except he'd go home to a lonely house every night rather than occasionally. But that was selfish. He needed to consider his children's welfare.

Martha continued, "Maybe we could do it for a trial period." She had a gleam in her eye that made Jonathan cringe. "You're still in mourning for several more months . . ."

Three months to be exact.

"Once the mourning period is over, you'd be free to think of remarrying. So what if we do this? We'll keep the children until you're ready to remarry. That way you can get your debt paid off and be ready for a fresh start."

But what if he chose not to remarry? He'd been unlucky in love twice already. He wasn't about to risk loving and losing again.

Martha knew enough to hold her own counsel as he mulled over his choices. Remarrying wasn't one of them. Perhaps, though, if he left the children with her, he could work in the greenhouse until late at night, grow more exotic crops, and pay off his debt faster. Then he wouldn't need to touch his emergency funds, so he'd have that available if the children needed anything or one of the animals required special care.

Whatever he decided, it would be painful. If he chose to pay off the debt, he'd only see his children for a short while in the early evenings. Once he made the money, he'd have to give up the produce business to spend time with his family. Tending plants called to his spirit and soothed his soul. He'd rather grow vegetables than work in the dairy business, but he doubted he could make enough money selling produce. Much as it would sadden him to give it up, he'd sacrifice anything to be with his children.

He rose from the chair. "Let me think about it, and I'll give you my decision tomorrow."

Martha sat forward on the sofa and opened her mouth to speak, but David shook his head and she subsided. Sitting back, she pressed her lips together, although her eyes seemed to be demanding an answer.

His voice thick, Jonathan said, "I'll go upstairs to say good night."

"I don't think—" Martha began, but David laid a hand on her arm. "Try not to wake them," she said softly.

Jonathan had no intention of waking them. Although he longed to snatch them out of their beds and carry them home, he'd let them sleep. As he mounted each step, the weight of his sorrow increased. He wasn't sure he could live his life knowing his little ones weren't his to care for anymore.

A lump in his throat, he opened the girls' bedroom door. Martha had fixed the room with matching heart quilts in pink and green. Even with the moonlight streaming through the window, he could barely make out the soft colors or his daughters' small bodies curled up underneath them. He sat on Libby's bed and laid a hand on her back. The soft rise and fall of her breath brought tears to his eyes. He hadn't seen her for two days and, with every fiber of his being, he wanted to gather her in his arms and cradle her close, but it wouldn't be fair to wake her. Laying a hand on her head, he whispered a prayer that God would protect her.

Then he stood and moved to Hannah's bed. He'd miss her most of all if he agreed to Martha's plan because she was his little shadow. She loved helping in the barn with the milking. Although she was too young to handle the equipment, she assisted with feeding the cows and sweeping the aisles, and she was learning to muck the stalls.

If ever there was a time for him to assert himself, this was it. He should demand custody of his own children, but something stopped him. He had to do what was best for them, no matter how hard it was for him.

Though he was grateful for all David and Martha had done, the children were his responsibility. He had to find a way to keep his family together.

4

The door clicked behind Rose with a finality that chilled her. Rejected. Shut out from her childhood home. Mamm and AnaMary were only a few feet away behind that closed door, but unreachable. An ache blossomed in Rose's chest, constricting her breathing.

She sank onto the porch steps, her suitcase beside her. She'd mentally prepared herself to face Daed's wrath, but the revulsion on his face and the disgust in his voice cut her to the core. Closing her eyes, she rubbed her forehead, wishing she could erase the words echoing in her ear.

She'd hoped Daed's physical frailty would have lessened some of his fight. His temper, though, hadn't changed. His rages no longer frightened her the way they had when she was child. As a nurse, she'd learned to defuse the anger of belligerent patients and to stand up for herself when necessary. But when she walked through the front door of her childhood home, part of her reverted to that long-ago Rose who was petrified.

The Rose who dreaded making mistakes, who cowered from blows, and who prayed to be rescued. Sometimes she woke in the night, covered in a film of sweat, panicked about a farm chore she'd left undone. Even now, if someone came up behind her unexpectedly, Rose flinched and shied away. The hospital staff had learned never to touch her shoulders from behind. Fingers on her shoulder brought back memories of that heavy hand clamping down, followed by swift and severe punishment.

Rose dug through her purse for her cell phone. Deep down, she'd been convinced she was making a mistake when she responded to AnaMary's letter, took time off work, and boarded the train. If she'd listened to the warning voice in her head, she never would have taken any of those steps. She'd lost a whole day of work and would lose one more, but she'd rectify her mistakes by heading back to New York. Back to where she belonged.

Relief washed over her as she clicked the cell phone button. No charge. *Oh, great.*

The phone shanty still stood in their neighbor's driveway, its paint peeling and wooden boards leaning to one side. Rose hesitated to approach the rickety building, but she needed to make her call and get out of here. She crossed the yards between the two houses, fighting the urge to look over her shoulder. Daed lay in bed, ill. He wouldn't burst from the front door.

The shanty door creaked and scraped against the ground, giving the impression it was used infrequently. Rose picked up the receiver, and the nausea she'd experienced that long-ago day flooded back. She relived every detail—her sweaty palms, her tight grip, and her terror of discovery. Even the chicken's beak pecking her arms. Closing her eyes, she tried to tamp down the spiraling fear.

She took a deep breath to calm herself and placed the receiver to her ear. The phone that had once been her lifeline was dead.

Now what?

The nearest farms on both sides were Amish. The chances of finding electricity or a phone were slim, and she needed to get out of here. Whom could she ask to take her to the station? Jonathan came to mind. As much as she disliked the thought of seeing him and Esther together, he seemed her only hope.

When they were younger, she and David had taken shortcuts

through the fields and woods. Rose couldn't bump her suitcase over that rough terrain, so she'd stick to the back roads. It'd take her an hour or more the long way around, but Jonathan should be done milking when she arrived. She hoped he'd be willing to take her into town to catch the train.

Dragging her suitcase behind her, Rose wound her way down the country lanes, letting the peace soak into her soul. She'd missed this serenity and slow pace. In New York, the relentless sirens, honking, banging, and clanking grated on her nerves. The knots of tension slowly unraveled until she arrived at Jonathan's house.

Hot, tired, and sweaty from the long walk, Rose clunked her suitcase up the steps to the porch. The knots retangled and pulled so tight, her stomach hurt. Gathering her courage, Rose knocked and waited. And waited some more. Perhaps they hadn't heard. She tried pounding harder. Still no answer. Perhaps Jonathan was still milking, although it seemed a bit late. Rose left her suitcase on the porch and rounded the house to the barn, where all the cows were in their stalls. The barn was immaculate, but empty of humans. The gardens and small greenhouse were bursting with plants, but no people.

Surely since Jonathan and Esther had young children, they'd be eating by now. Or even putting the children down to bed. Could they be visiting? If so, they'd be coming home soon. Farmers who got up at four to milk went to bed with the sun.

Rose headed for the front porch and sat on a rocker. Exhaustion overtook her. Nervousness and fear had kept her up most of last night, and then she'd risen at dawn to take the subway to the station. The long train ride, worrying about Mamm and AnaMary, being in her family home, reliving the nightmare in the phone shanty, and Daed's rage—all of it had drained her.

She closed her eyes and drifted off into daydreams. She and Jonathan were strolling hand in hand when a buggy rattled into the driveway, startling her back to reality.

Every fiber of Jonathan's being was fatigued from waging an internal battle. Martha's plan made sense, but there had to be a better way to keep his family together. By the time he arrived at home, he was no closer to a solution than he had been in his brother's living room. He pulled into the driveway, dreading another long and sleepless night.

A shape shifted on his front porch, and his senses jumped to high alert. Someone was hidden in the shadows. He slowed the buggy. Who would be here this time of night? Or was it an animal?

No, a woman stood beside one of the rockers. As soon as she headed toward the porch steps, he recognized her. Rose. The old yearning overwhelmed him. He'd seen her on this porch of his childhood home many times, waiting for his brother David, and each time desire had surged through him. Although it had been seven years since he'd seen her, that hadn't changed. To calm his racing pulse, he reminded himself her Amish dress was a sham.

Jonathan stopped the buggy and climbed out. "Rose? What are you doing here this time of night?" As soon as he said the words, he wished he hadn't. The slump of her shoulders and forced smile told him the reason. Her Daed must have refused to let her into the house.

Rose descended the steps, and the moonlight highlighting her features increased his longing. He forced himself to look away.

"I need to get to the station. I wanted to call a taxi, but my phone is dead."

He would have offered to let her use his business phone in the barn, but there was no point in calling now. Even if he drove her, the last train would have left. "You planned to go to the station at this time of night?"

She bit her lip and glanced up at the night sky as if confused. "I'm sorry. I didn't realize it was so late. I stopped by earlier, but I must have fallen asleep." She turned her back and headed for the porch. "I'll just get my suitcase and go."

"Rose, wait."

At his words, she turned and faced him, her eyes filled with distress. He wanted to gather her into his arms and comfort her.

"Where are you planning to go?"

She shrugged and didn't meet his eyes. Jonathan wished he could invite her into his house. Having her there might ease the loneliness of the empty house, but that would be wrong. In so many ways.

"I'd offer to take you to the station, but it's too late to catch a train now."

He wracked his brains to think of a way to help her. Everyone nearby would be asleep. The only place she might be able to spend the night was Martha and David's house. Jonathan hated to wake them up, knowing that Martha would be up most of the night with the baby. He had no idea how David would react to seeing his ex-girlfriend. Or if it would bring up Martha's jealousy over David's love for Rose, old feelings Jonathan suspected had never died. And he wasn't sure either of them would welcome Rose after the trouble she'd caused.

"Please don't worry about me." Rose climbed the porch steps. "I'll figure out something."

Jonathan followed her up the stairs. "Here, let me get your suitcase." She stepped back and let him pick it up, but being this close to her made it hard to breathe. He gestured toward the buggy. "I'll take you to David and Martha's."

"David and . . . Martha?"

Rose's expression indicated her shock and what seemed to be disapproval. Did it bother her that David had married someone else? She certainly hadn't expected David to wait for her, had she? Not when she'd left him without a word.

"My children are sleeping there tonight." Jonathan hoped it was only for the night, but if he agreed to Martha's idea . . . He'd think about that later.

A strange look crossed Rose's face—panic, maybe?—before she said, "I don't think that's a good idea."

Jonathan didn't think it was either, but what other choices did they have? "It's much too late to wake the neighbors," he pointed out.

"Of course, but we'll be disturbing Martha and . . . David."

The way she'd hesitated before saying David's name made Jonathan wonder if she still harbored feelings for his brother. The thought made his stomach clench. He motioned for her to precede him down the steps. "Martha may still be up caring for Amos. He's been teething."

"If you're sure . . ."

No, he wasn't sure at all, but he couldn't leave Rose stranded. "Martha won't mind. She's like her namesake in the Bible—always helping others." He had no idea how she'd feel about aiding Rose and only hoped Christian charity would prevail.

They arrived at the buggy and Jonathan reached out to assist her, but jerked his hand back before he made contact. He shouldn't be touching her. He needed to avoid temptation. Besides, he was still in his mourning period, and even if he weren't, Rose had left the Amish. They had no future together.

"I know all about Martha's gift of hospitality." Rose climbed into the buggy. "It's just, well, awkward coming back after all these years."

"I can imagine," Jonathan said as he slid the passenger door closed.

Rose must be carrying a huge load of guilt as well. Everyone had forgiven her as God commanded, but Jonathan suspected that seeing Rose would be painful for all of them.

Rose breathed more easily once Jonathan closed the door and went to the back of the buggy to stow her suitcase. His nearness made it hard to relax. She only hoped she hadn't given away her feelings. And for a short a while, she could even manage to think.

So David had married her best friend, Martha? Rose had trouble picturing the two of them together. Although David and Rose had never officially started courting, they spent so much time together while they were growing up, people automatically assumed they'd be a couple once they joined the church. And they would have been, if Rose hadn't run away.

But David and Martha had never gotten along well. Rose wondered how they ended up courting. They seemed an unlikely couple.

The buggy tilted slightly as Jonathan got in the other side. His presence filled the confined space. She sucked in a quick gulp of air as he settled next to her and picked up the reins, his arm nearly brushing hers.

"Rose?" Jonathan tilted his head in the way that always made her feel he was waiting breathlessly for her answer. "Are you all right?"

Rose wasn't sure. Plunging back into the past had thrown off her equilibrium, and sitting this close to Jonathan . . . No words could describe what that was doing to her.

"I'm just tired," she mumbled. That was the truth, but not the whole truth. She couldn't say the rest of it. *I'm imagining myself in your arms, cradled against your chest.*

"I guess it was a long trip." Jonathan jiggled the reins and the horse started off.

"Yes, and seeing Mamm and AnaMary was hard. And Daed . . ." Rose choked up.

Jonathan turned the horse, and they started down the dark roads. "How did that go?" His quiet question sounded sympathetic, and he kept his gaze on the road rather than on her, which made it a little easier to answer.

"He was upset." *Upset* was too mild a word to describe Daed's reaction. "Furious, really. He ordered me out of the house. I'd hoped"—she clasped her hands together to keep them from shaking—"he'd be too ill to protest."

"He hasn't forgiven you for leaving?"

"No, and I don't think he ever will."

Overhead, the clouds slid in front of the moon, blocking the pale light that had illuminated Jonathan's face and plunging them into blackness. A blackness that matched the darkness in her soul. As her eyes adjusted, she could pick out the faint outline of his face and body. All those years ago, she'd not only lost her family, she'd also lost Jonathan.

"Oh, Rose." Jonathan's large warm hand enveloped hers. "I'm sorry."

Strength flowed from his hand to hers, and Rose was grateful for that lifeline on such a troubling day. They rode in silence for a while, with only the rattle and squeak of the wheels and the night sounds surrounding them.

The almost-full moon peeped from behind the clouds. That and Jonathan's hand holding hers gave her a sliver of hope.

Jonathan gave her hand a quick squeeze and let go. "It's probably none of my business, but what made you leave?"

Rose thought she detected an undercurrent of sadness in his words, but that was nothing compared to hers. She couldn't tell him the real reason she'd fled—she'd been in love with him, and his engagement to Esther had broken her heart.

She'd also needed to escape from her family. Rose didn't want to share either explanation, but she had to say something, or he might guess it was connected with him. She'd left the day after he and Esther had gotten engaged. Until then she'd hoped he might change his mind.

"Things had gotten tense with Daed. He started exploding over the tiniest mistakes. And as for the large ones—"

"Did he—" Jonathan's hands tightened on the reins. "Did he hurt you?"

Rose remained silent as memories scrolled past. Daed's furious face inches from hers, his hands gripping her shoulder. "Sometimes," she admitted. "But mostly he hurt me with his temper and his words."

Jonathan made a low, growling sound deep in his throat. "I wish I'd known. I would have found a way to protect you."

To know that he cared warmed Rose inside and out. "Thank you," she whispered, but then guilt took its place. He was a married man. For him the hand squeeze and offer of protection were only chivalry. She wanted to build them into something more, something that could never be.

"We were all so concerned about you when you left. How did you manage to survive in the Englisch world?"

"It was hard. I had so much to learn. But my cousin gave me a phone number to call and the Amish Descendant Scholarship Fund paid for my education so I could graduate from nurses' training."

"So you like nursing then and living in New York?"

"Yes, I love helping people, and although I miss the peacefulness of this"—she waved a hand in the direction of the farmland they were passing—"I've gotten used to city life."

"I see."

Jonathan looked disappointed, but of course, he would be. Anyone Amish would be bothered by her decision to leave the community and the faith. They wouldn't understand that she still did her best to follow her faith even when she was living in the world.

He cleared his throat. "So you wouldn't consider coming back?"

"I'm content where I am." Rose wanted to end any discussion of her returning to the community. If she stayed overnight here, no doubt Martha and David also would try to talk her into staying and joining the church.

5

Jonathan tapped lightly at the door and a few minutes later, Martha opened it a crack, her hair frizzing out from her braid. She clutched a wrap tightly around her, hiding her nightgown. Her dazed eyes made it clear he'd woken her from a deep sleep, which filled him with guilt.

"Did you forget something?" she asked.

"No. I hate to ask another favor after you've done so much already—" Martha interrupted him. "You know we'd do anything for you."

Including offering Rose shelter for the night?

He thought that Martha might regret her generosity when she realized what he planned to ask her.

Jonathan reached for Rose's elbow and drew her closer to the door. Martha, one side of her face turned away, stared blearily for a moment. Then her eyes widened, and she staggered back a few steps. "R-Rose?"

Rose shook off Jonathan's hand on her arm, and before he could stop her, she stepped forward, arms outstretched. "Hi, Martha. Jonathan insisted we come. I hope we didn't wake you."

Martha's eyes blazed as she glared at Jonathan, and she leaned against the door, as if to slam it in their faces. He placed a hand on the door and pushed to keep it from closing. "Martha, please. Rose has nowhere to sleep tonight."

His sister-in-law said nothing, only stared at him as if he'd betrayed her. Jonathan tried to apologize with his eyes. "She came home to care for her ill Daed, but he kicked her out of the house." He hoped Rose's distress would bring out Martha's caring nature. He guessed right.

She opened the door but stood behind it. "Come in," she said gruffly.

Jonathan started to motion for Rose to go in first when he spied the glint of tears. Was she hurt by Martha's coldness? From the way she was looking at him, it seemed she, too, was upset with him.

"I didn't want her to know about Daed. Now she'll pity me." Rose nibbled at her lower lip. "It also doesn't seem like she wants me here."

That was an understatement, but Jonathan had gotten Martha to open the door. He wasn't about to lose this opportunity. Where else could Rose find shelter at this time of night?

"Are you coming in?" Martha remained hidden behind the door, but Jonathan could sense her displeasure.

And now Rose seemed on the verge of refusing to enter. In a few short minutes, he'd managed to upset two women he cared about.

"Please, Rose?" Jonathan motioned toward the open doorway. To his relief, she stepped over the threshold. He followed her inside.

Martha shut the door behind them and leaned against it, taking several deep breaths before she said, "The small back bedroom upstairs is empty. The girls are in the front room. Amos's crib is in the middle bedroom, but he's sleeping in the cradle in our room down here." She turned slightly so only the good side of her profile was visible.

"Do you think you can find your way?" Jonathan asked Rose. When she nodded, he headed toward the door. "I'll bring in your suitcase, and I'll pick you up early tomorrow morning right after milking and breakfast. Say about seven?"

"How do you plan to get all your work done tomorrow?" Martha put her hands on her hips. "You can barely complete everything as it is."

"There's always time in the day to help others." Jonathan hoped she didn't think he was judging her. To soften his words, he added, "You certainly manage to find many hours in the day to help my family."

Her lips curved in a half smile that she quickly subdued, probably because she didn't want to appear proud. *Hochmut* was a sin.

"I hope the baby doesn't wake you," Martha said. "He's up a lot during the night, so I try to sleep whenever he does."

"I'm so sorry we woke you," Rose said.

Martha nodded but didn't reply.

Jonathan sighed inwardly. Martha was doing her best to make Rose feel unwelcome. Although he understood why, he still ached for Rose. She'd just been rejected by her father; she didn't need more unkindness in addition to that hurt.

He opened the front door. "I'll be right back so everyone can get in bed."

"Everyone except you." Martha shook her head. "Heading home this late and you having to get up at four for the milking."

"I'll be fine." After all, he barely slept most nights anyway. Having something to do came as a welcome relief.

After the door shut behind Jonathan, Rose tried to make amends. "I apologize again for interrupting your sleep. It's so good to see you." When Martha only grunted, Rose continued, "You're looking well."

"Really?" Martha whirled to face Rose, revealing the misshapen, oddly colored, patched side of her face.

Rose bit back a gasp. One whole side of Martha's face had a skin graft. What had happened to her friend? Rose didn't want to ask because the bitterness in Martha's tone indicated it was a touchy subject, but she didn't want to ignore something that bothered Martha deeply. Rose gestured vaguely in the direction of Martha's burns. "I'm very sorry . . ."

"You should be," Martha snapped.

Had Martha understood Rose was referring to the skin graft? Or did she think Rose meant about leaving the Amish?

Martha turned her back on Rose and pulled the curtain to one side. "You're taking advantage of him. Do you have any idea how far behind you'll put him on his work if he drives you into town?"

Rose clutched the sides of her skirt to release some of her frustration. "I don't want to be a burden."

"Then tell him you'll wait until he does his next delivery. He has restaurants near the train station."

"But I . . ."

"What?" Martha turned around and pinned her with a glare. "You can't stay away from your Englisch job that long?"

Martha's disgusted look made Rose long to defend herself. Now that she was no longer Amish, she didn't have to worry about Hochmut, but something inside her rebelled against following Englisch customs of bragging or contradicting others to make herself feel better or superior.

Rose tried not to let her irritation show on her face or in her words. "I have the week off."

"Perhaps you should consider staying here the whole time. You could attend church and make peace with those you've hurt."

Martha made it sound as if Rose had hurt many people. So far as she knew, she'd hurt her family by running away, and possibly David, if he'd been considering her as a future wife. Martha surely wouldn't expect her to apologize to David. If Rose had stayed, he and Martha never would have married. Rose wanted to point that out but held her peace. Martha had enough hostility toward her already.

Rose fished around in her purse. "I could leave sooner if I could get a charge for my cell pho—"

Martha was staring at the phone in Rose's hand as if it were a snake about to bite. Evidently, she wasn't one of the Amish who were using cell phones.

Rose dropped it back in her purse. Perhaps she could find somewhere to do that tomorrow.

The door opened, and Jonathan entered carrying the suitcase. He looked from one to the other. "Is everything all right?"

Between Martha's glower and Rose's desire to bolt, he must have sensed the undercurrents running through the room. If she were honest, Rose couldn't answer yes.

When nobody answered, Jonathan walked to the steps and picked up the battery-powered lantern on the newel post. "I'll take Rose's suitcase up and be right back." Then he turned to Rose. "Would you like me to show you the room?"

Rose agreed, but Martha said, "No need. I can do that."

Jonathan's understanding glance made Rose wish he were looking at her. "I know you can, and I also know you need your sleep. I'll make sure Rose knows which room it is."

Martha looked as if she wanted to protest, but she clamped her mouth shut. Jonathan and Rose were partway up the stairs when Martha said, "Rose has agreed to stay several days, so you don't need to worry about driving her to the station tomorrow. She said she'll go whenever you need to make your next deliveries."

Rose stared at her openmouthed. After the way Martha had been acting, why would she want Rose to stay? And she hadn't agreed to that, had she? She almost protested, but the relief on Jonathan's face stopped her.

"That would be great." Jonathan turned and smiled a smile that could easily entice Rose to stay here forever.

They mounted the stairs and trod softly down the hall to a small room. Jonathan shone the light around the room to show her the furnishings, and Rose blinked back tears. Simple and sturdy, these pieces had been in Martha's childhood bedroom. Rose had sometimes spent the night in this bed with the same pinwheel quilt. The two of them had whispered together late at night, sharing secrets.

Back then, they never would have dreamed of where they'd ended up today: Rose no longer Amish, and her two best friends, Martha and David, who had heartily disliked each other, now married. One secret from back then she'd never shared with Martha—or anyone—was the crush she had on Jonathan.

He set the suitcase at the foot of the bed. "Are you all right?"

Could he detect the glint of tears in her eyes? "I'll be fine." She thanked him for the ride and for carrying up the suitcase without looking up at him, both to hide her tears and to avoid revealing her feelings.

After he said a hasty good night and left the room, Rose started to close the door, but she couldn't resist staring at him as he hurried down the hall. He clicked off the lantern and eased open the door of the front bedroom. He stayed in there for a while, and when he came out, his head was bowed and he rubbed his eyes. Rose ducked behind the door so he wouldn't see her. After he went downstairs, she shut the door.

Enough moonlight streamed into the room so Rose could find her nightgown, and she fell into bed exhausted, her mind whirling. Since she left New York this morning, she'd seen her family for the first time in seven years, but then she had been ordered out of their home. She'd ridden with the man she loved, only to discover he was married and had three children. She'd reconnected with her best friend from childhood, who'd been badly scarred and seemed to be filled with animosity. Martha had always been rather blunt, but tonight she'd gone out of her way to be unkind. Was she upset about Rose leaving the Amish? Or was there another reason? And why had she issued an invitation to stay?

After dropping off Rose's suitcase, Jonathan left the room as quickly as possible. Being there with her in the dark was too tempting. He longed to take her in his arms, hold her close. On the way downstairs, he stopped to check on the girls. He turned off the lantern, tiptoed into the room, and stood silent as their small chests rose and fell with each soft breath. Moonbeams illuminated their angelic faces, and his chest constricted. If he agreed to Martha's plan, nights like this would be the only time he'd see his precious daughters.

Kneeling between their beds, he prayed God's blessing on each of his children and asked for guidance in keeping them together as a family. Then he pressed a kiss to Hannah's and Libby's foreheads before he left the room. He wished Amos were sleeping in his crib up here so he could look in at his son.

Heaviness weighed down his spirit as he shut the bedroom door. Heading back to his empty house would be even harder tonight without Hannah's company, and his loneliness increased after spending time with Rose. The hole left by Esther's passing had enlarged. Why had God brought Rose back into his life to stir those old memories and longings he'd suppressed? Her masquerading as Amish made it even harder to separate dreams from reality.

Jonathan slipped down the stairs without turning on the lantern so he wouldn't disturb Martha, David, and Amos in the downstairs bedroom. He set the lantern on the newel post, where Martha kept it, and headed for the front door.

"It's about time." Martha's voice, low and sarcastic, came from the darkness behind him. "It shouldn't take that long to carry a suitcase down the hall. I was just about to come up and check on you."

Jonathan turned, debating whether he should explain or ignore the gibe. Martha already had built up animosity toward Rose, so he felt he should defend Rose's reputation. "The suitcase took only a few seconds. I wanted to check on the girls, then I spent some time in prayer about the decision I need to make tomorrow."

Martha drew in a breath. "Oh. I'm sorry for being so *gretzy*. I'm overtired from the night feedings, but I shouldn't take it out on you."

"Or on Rose," Jonathan said.

"Rose is different." Martha ran her fingertips over the skin graft, a nervous motion she often used when she was tired or upset.

"Can't you forgive her and let the past go?"

Martha shook her head. "It's not that easy. Most offenses I can forgive immediately, but this has festered for so long and runs so deep."

Jonathan waved a hand in the direction of the upstairs bedroom. "You have her here under your roof for the next few days. Why not use that time to make your peace?"

6

Yawning, Rose stretched out on the bed, but sleep refused to come. Memories of the past haunted her. How many times had she and Martha confided in each other in a bedroom that held this furniture? Martha was the only one outside the family who knew of Daed's hot temper and Rose's fears. Martha was the one Rose had trusted with her goodbye note when she left the Amish. So why was her childhood friend so negative toward her now?

Rose tossed and turned as her thoughts raced and collided. Memories of Martha led to David and then Jonathan. Rose depleted most of her energy trying to keep thoughts of Jonathan from overtaking her mind and emotions, but the more she pushed those thoughts away, the more insistent they became. When she finally did drift off, she was in Jonathan's arms.

She woke, disoriented, in the middle of the night. She leaped out of bed, convinced she was at work and the wailing baby was her responsibility. It took a while to remember where she was and calm her racing heart. Rose debated about going downstairs to help Martha but suspected her childhood friend might resent her interference.

She crawled back into bed, unclenched her teeth and fists, and forced herself to relax. Her natural instinct was to run to help anyone in distress, but tonight she had to leave the comforting to someone else. She finally fell back to sleep, only to be reawakened an hour later by more loud cries. Again, she made herself lie in bed and let Martha deal with it, but when the bawling occurred a few hours after that, the pull to hold the crying infant became irresistible. Rose slipped on her clothes in case she ran into David and hurried downstairs to find Martha, her hair in disarray, her eyes bloodshot and puffy, stumbling along, patting Amos's back.

"Can I help?" she asked softly.

Martha jumped and turned startled eyes in Rose's direction. She hugged the baby to her and cowered as if afraid Rose might hurt Amos or take him away.

What did Martha think Rose would do to the little boy? She wouldn't try to influence the children to turn Englisch, if that's what her friend was worried about. For heaven's sake, the baby wasn't even a year old yet. Being held by an Englischer certainly wouldn't hurt him.

Rose adopted the manner she used to soothe worried patients. "I'd be happy to take him from you so you can get some rest." She held out her arms. "You must be exhausted."

"No!" Martha's sharp tone cut Rose deeply.

Rose stepped closer, but Martha backed away. "I'm a nurse," Rose assured her, "and I've had pediatric training."

"Not that I have any idea what that means, but it doesn't change the fact I can't trust you to care for Amos." Martha clutched the baby even more tightly and turned her back as if sheltering him from Rose.

"It means I took special classes in caring for babies and children."

"Book learning only goes so far."

Rose stopped herself before she explained she'd taken care of plenty of infants in the hospital. Martha would only consider it bragging or perhaps think Rose was criticizing her care of Amos. Maybe Martha was insecure about her child-rearing skills and worried that Rose would show her up.

Once again, Martha had made Rose feel she needed to defend herself. Why was she on the defensive around her friend—or should she consider Martha a former friend? For some reason, Martha almost seemed to view Rose as an enemy.

Rose trudged upstairs, hurt by the way Martha had rebuffed her efforts to help with the baby and sorry she'd agreed to stay here for the next few days.

No one in the Amish community would support Rose's turning Englisch, but they wouldn't shun her. If Rose had joined the church and then left the Amish, she'd understand being shunned. But she'd left before starting baptismal classes, so why were people treating her as if she were an outcast? She drifted off to sleep before she could answer that question.

Someone tugged at her covers, startling Rose awake. She rolled over to find a small girl with her eyes half-closed and tears rolling down her cheeks, struggling to climb into her bed. She reached down and gathered the small girl into her arms. She'd brave Martha's wrath to comfort the child.

The little girl snuggled against her, and Rose warmed to the sweetness of cuddling a child. She'd always longed to be a mother, but that would never be. She refused to date an Englischer, and no Amish man could ask her to be his wife unless she joined the church. Rose ached inside that she'd miss out on holding her own little ones. In her drowsiness, Rose pretended she was cradling her own daughter, and in that dreamland, Jonathan smiled down at both of them.

Earsplitting shrieks resounded through the upstairs. Rose jolted upright in bed and almost dislodged the small girl curled up beside her. Every nerve on alert, Rose laid a gentle hand on the child to keep her sleeping while she jumped out of bed. As a nurse, she was used to responding to emergencies, and the screams—from an adult rather than an infant this time—seemed to be coming from the front bedroom.

She burst into the room to find Martha sitting on the edge of an unmade bed, weeping. The little girl on the matching twin bed sat with her back pressed against the wall, her eyes wide and frightened. Rose longed to comfort the child, but Martha had been screaming. Rose went over and laid a hand on Martha's shoulder. Martha gulped in air and twisted away.

"Are you all right? Do you hurt anywhere?" Rose scanned her for signs of bleeding but noticed nothing out of the ordinary.

"I . . . looked . . . everywhere . . ." Martha was hyperventilating.

Rose put on her authoritative nursing persona. "Breathe in slowly and deeply . . . keep going . . . a little more. Now exhale slowly . . . Keep blowing out your breath . . . That's it. More. Let's do it again."

Amazingly, Martha responded and did as Rose asked until her breathing calmed to a slower level.

Once it had, Rose asked again, "Are you hurt?" Martha shook her head, and Rose followed up. "What's wrong?"

Martha wrung her hands. "Jonathan will never let me—" She buried her face in her hands. A sob escaped her.

"What won't Jonathan let you do?" Rose was trying to make sense of Martha's broken narrative. She seemed to have lost something that would upset Jonathan. From what Rose had seen growing up, Jonathan never worried over lost possessions. Perhaps he'd changed, or maybe Martha was overwrought from lack of sleep.

"Take care of the children." Martha hung her head. "Not with Hannah missing."

"Hannah?" Rose's stomach churned. "Is she a blonde about four years old?"

"Yes." Martha clutched at her arm. "You've seen her?"

"She's asleep in the bed in the back bedroom." Although how Hannah had managed to sleep through all the noise baffled Rose.

"You took her out of her bed?" Martha screeched. "And let me think she'd disappeared?" She jumped to her feet, raced down the hall, and shoved open the bedroom door.

The door flew in a wide arc and hit the wall with a bang that woke Hannah. She jumped and sat upright in bed, her chin quivering.

Martha sagged against the doorframe. Rose wanted to comfort Hannah, but Martha was blocking the entrance. She tried to convey a calming message, and Hannah looked from Martha to Rose and back again.

"What are you doing in here?" Martha demanded. "You should be in your own bed. You scared me half to death."

Rose tried to take the pressure off Hannah, who looked about to burst into tears. "I think she was sleepwalking or had a bad dream."

Martha whirled. "Then you should have put her back in her own bed."

"I'm sorry. I didn't think about looking for her room."

"Exactly. That's why I can't trust you around the children."

The sun had barely peeked over the horizon, and already the morning was off to a bad start. She'd been hoping to make a fresh start and get in Martha's good graces this morning, but she'd failed miserably. When they were younger, Martha had always had a tendency to worry, but she'd never been this nervous. Perhaps dealing with three small children and not getting enough sleep had made her nerves worse.

Jonathan knocked on his brother's door early in the morning. Part of him told him it was foolishness when he had so much work to do, but he missed his children. He hadn't seen them last night, and he wouldn't see them until dinnertime. He'd endured a lonely night without Hannah's company and again this morning as he did the milking without her by his side. He pushed aside the niggling thought that he also wanted to see Rose.

The minute he'd recognized Rose yesterday, seven years vanished in an instant, and he was back to the past, when he'd admired her from afar. That hadn't changed. He was still acutely aware of her presence. The same way he'd always been whenever she entered the room. Flashes of her smile, her eyes meeting his, her bell-like laughter . . .

"Jonathan?" Martha's eyes widened. "What are you doing here?" Her cheeks colored. "I'm sorry. I didn't mean you weren't welcome." She opened the door and motioned for him to enter. "You're never here this early in the day. Is anything wrong?"

"Everything's fine. I missed the children because I didn't get to see them last night." He tried not to let his frustration come through in his words.

"Oh." That one word held worlds of meaning, including guilt, which was also reflected on her face.

Jonathan hadn't been trying to make her feel bad. "I'll just say hello to everyone. Then I have to get back to work."

Martha closed the door behind him. "Amos is still sleeping, but the girls are in the kitchen."

"I'll peek in on Amos first."

She scurried ahead of him and eased open the bedroom door. "Try not to wake him," she whispered.

Jonathan tiptoed across the wide plank floor to his son's crib. He clenched his hands into fists to prevent himself from smoothing back the curls on Amos's head. All he wanted to do was scoop his son into his arms and cradle him close. How long had it been since he'd done that?

Choking back the lump in his throat, he prayed for his son. Then he rejoined Martha in the doorway and took one last glimpse before she shut the door.

Jonathan turned to her. "How was he last night?"

"As well as can be expected." Martha led the way to the kitchen.

In other words, it must have been a rough night. "So he woke up a lot?"

"A little."

The circles under Martha's bleary eyes indicated differently, but Jonathan didn't question her too closely. She got prickly whenever she believed anyone was questioning her competence.

Jonathan took a deep breath. "Something smells delicious."

"The breakfast casserole is almost ready to come out of the oven. I'll set another place for you."

"No, I won't be staying. I have too much work to do."

The minute he walked through the doorway, Hannah squealed. She jumped up from the table and raced toward him. He knelt and opened his arms. She collided with his chest, almost knocking him over. Wrapping his arms around her, he stood, reveling in their closeness.

Libby smiled at him from across the table. She was much quieter and shier than Hannah.

He went around the table and squatted beside her, shifting Hannah to one side. "Can I have a hug?"

Libby's grin widened, and she threw her arms around his neck. He lifted her into his arms and, one girl on each side, he glanced across the table at Rose. He wasn't certain, but her eyes seemed to be glinting with tears.

Their gazes locked, and Jonathan drowned in her green eyes. He might have stayed mesmerized if the oven door hadn't banged behind him.

Martha bustled to the table with the egg casserole. The heady aroma of bacon, cheese, and pepper made his mouth water, but he had work to do. He set his daughters in their places.

"Tell David I'll see him this evening." He turned to go but couldn't resist one last glance at Rose, who was seated beside Hannah. He kept it brief so Martha wouldn't notice.

"Let me cut you a piece of this to take along," Martha said. "If I know you, you'll forget to eat."

Jonathan waited while she cut and wrapped a generous slice, grateful because it gave him more time to study Rose, who had her head bent to hear something Hannah was whispering. That long-ago yearning snaked through his chest. *She'd make a wonderful mother.* Thoughts of her courting an Englischer made his stomach roil. If only she hadn't left the Amish.

"Here." Martha nudged him.

Jonathan turned his attention to her. How long had she been standing there, holding out the foil-wrapped package? He hoped it appeared he'd been gazing at Hannah rather than Rose. With a thank-you to Martha and a quick wave to his girls, Jonathan headed from the kitchen.

"Daed!" Hannah hopped up from the table and ran after him. Tackling him around the knees, she begged, "Take me with you."

Jonathan steeled himself. "Not today, Hannah. I have too much work to do. You stay here with your Aenti." As much as he loved having her with him, he needed to make up for all the work he'd missed yesterday doing deliveries and driving Rose.

When she looked up at him with tears in her eyes, he almost crumbled. How could he say no to that sweet face with her trembling lips and pleading eyes? Before he could agree, Martha hurried into the room, swooped down, and lifted Hannah into her arms.

"Your Daed needs to work." She headed toward the kitchen with a struggling, crying Hannah wriggling in her arms. "Don't worry. He'll be back for dinner."

"Be good for Martha, Hannah," Jonathan said as Martha carried his daughter through the kitchen doorway. He put a hand on the doorknob and let himself out the front door while her sobs issued from the kitchen, breaking his heart.

7

Martha plopped Hannah on the bench beside Rose, and Rose put an arm around her shoulder. Hannah buried her face against Rose's chest.

"Better not to coddle her," Martha said. "She needs to get used to being separated from her Daed."

Rose longed to ask why, but the tight lines etched into Martha's face made her look forbidding. Perhaps it would be best to wait for another time. With Martha glaring at her, Rose tried to disengage Hannah's arms gently, but Hannah only clung more tightly.

"Maybe she needs a little time to get over it," Rose suggested.

"Crying won't change the situation, though."

Martha's clenched jaw and rigid shoulders signaled that perhaps she could use a good cry herself, but Rose kept that thought to herself.

"Crying can release sadness and tension."

Martha whirled around as the back door opened.

David stepped through carrying a metal milk can. He stopped and studied Martha's face. "What's wrong?"

"Nothing." She bent to lift the can and poured some into a pitcher she set at the table.

When she set it down, David moved around behind her and kneaded her shoulders. "Rough night?"

Most Amish couples didn't show affection in front of others, so David massaging Martha's shoulders surprised Rose, but she was glad to see how much they cared about each other. She'd sometimes wondered if David had courted someone else, although she never would have guessed he'd choose Martha.

Despite her stance against it, Martha sounded about ready to cry. "Amos was up three times. Oh, and while you were sleeping, we had company. I wanted to tell you this morning before the milking, but I didn't hear you get up."

"I slipped out of bed quietly so I wouldn't disturb you or Amos. So what's this about company?" He turned, and his face whitened. "R-Rose?"

If she had any doubts that she'd broken his heart, the evidence was written plainly on his face for everyone to see, including Martha. He shuttered his feelings almost instantly, but his jerky gait and his furtive glances showed her presence had affected him.

"I'll wash up." He headed out of the kitchen, and Martha followed him.

Hannah was still sobbing silently, her chest heaving, so Rose gathered her close and stroked her cheek while Martha was out of the room.

Just outside the kitchen, David and Martha spoke in whispers, but their words carried into the kitchen.

"What's Rose doing here?"

"Jonathan dropped her off last night. Supposedly she came home to take care of her Daed, but he refused to let her into the house. She had nowhere to go last night, so I took her in."

"She's returning to the Amish?"

"No, as far as I know she's heading back to New York."

David's sigh was long and drawn out. "So she's leaving today?"

"*No* . . . Actually, I suggested she stay until Jonathan goes into town later this week."

"What were you thinking?" David words were panicky.

"That Jonathan is overworked and needs someone to watch out for him." Martha's quick answer sounded defensive.

"That was thoughtful of you."

Their voices faded as they moved down the hall.

When Hannah's sobs lessened to sniffles, Rose hugged her. "Feeling better?"

Martha's footsteps hurried down the hall to the kitchen, and Hannah sat up. She shook her head, her eyes still shiny with tears. "I miss my Daed."

"He has work to do, but he'll be back later, right?"

"Yes. I want my Mamm too."

Things had been so hectic since she arrived, Rose hadn't had a chance to inquire about Esther. "Where is your Mamm?"

Hannah's eyes brimmed with tears. "She's in—"

Martha burst through the door. "We've had enough crying for one day. Let's change the subject." With a warning glance at Rose, she said, "I'd appreciate it if you didn't stir up trouble. Things are hard enough around here without—" She broke off abruptly when David walked through the door.

"Is everything all right?" He glanced from one to the other, this time with a neutral look on his face when his eyes met Rose's.

"With all the interruptions this morning," Martha said, "I'm afraid the casserole is barely lukewarm." She set pieces on each plate.

Hannah shrank in her seat and leaned against Rose. "My tummy hurts."

"Most likely from too much crying." Martha sat at the table. "Sit up straight and eat every bite."

Rose had been in the Englisch world so long she'd forgotten the Amish rule of eating everything on the plate. When she first moved to New York, she'd been horrified when fellow nurses ordered meals and left half the food on their plates. She gradually got used to it, but walking back into an Amish household again, she reverted to childhood habits.

Everyone bowed their heads for silent prayer. When Rose lifted her head, Hannah's distress made her want to help the little girl. Rose's father had thundered at her whenever she picked at her meal. She waited until Martha leaned over to cut Libby's meal into small bites, and then she forked a large bite of Hannah's casserole into her own mouth. The small girl shot her a grateful glance.

Martha returned to her own plate, and everyone ate in silence. Rose wondered if they normally did or if the uncomfortable silence was related to her presence. Libby tipped over her milk. David reached out to right the glass, and Martha hopped up from the table to get a rag. Again, Rose ate a few more bites from Hannah's plate.

David turned in her direction, and his eyebrows rose as he stared at Hannah's almost-empty plate and Rose's full one, but to Rose's relief, he didn't say a word.

By the time Martha cleaned up the spill and settled into her chair again, Rose had managed to eat some of her own portion. Hannah stabbed at the small bit of casserole on her plate.

"Stop picking and eat," Martha ordered.

Rose reached for Hannah's left hand under the table and squeezed it. The small girl looked up at her with damp eyes, and Rose smiled in sympathy.

Martha huffed. "I wish you wouldn't encourage her."

David cleared his throat, and Martha looked at him. After his slight head shake, Martha stared down at her plate and ate her breakfast in silence.

Rose let go of Hannah's hand and finished her own meal as quickly as she could. Several times she almost asked a question or started a conversation, but Martha's sullen expression discouraged interactions.

Finally, David broke the tension. "So, Rose, you're a New Yorker now?"

"Yes, city life was an adjustment, but I'm used to it now."

"I see," David said. "Are you planning to stay here?"

He already knew the answer, so why did he ask? To encourage her to rethink her decision? Rose set her fork down on her plate. "No, I'm a nurse in New York, and I need to go back to work. I took some time off." To care for a father who didn't want her help.

Martha pointed to the few small bits remaining on Hannah's plate. "I expect you to clean off every bite."

Hannah picked up her fork and slid the last few bites into her mouth.

"See, that wasn't so bad, was it?" Martha stood and began clearing the table.

Rose got up to help her, but as soon as she picked up the plates, Martha took them from her. "I'll take care of that."

"I don't mind helping."

"I don't need help." Martha amended her remark with more measured tones when David raised his brows. "I can handle it. You're a guest. Just relax and enjoy yourself."

Rose had no idea how she could enjoy herself when Martha clearly didn't want her there, but when she sat again, Hannah reached for her hand under the table. Rose tucked the little girl's hand in hers and was rewarded with a sweet smile.

David pushed back his chair. "Thank you for a wonderful *gut* breakfast, Martha. Good to see you again, Rose." He started toward the back door. "I have a lot of work to do."

Once the dishes and table had been washed, Martha called the girls to her. Libby winced as Martha braided her chin-length hair into short pigtails. When Martha turned to Hannah, Amos began to cry. Martha set the brush on the table and hurried from the room.

Rose picked up the brush. "Shall I do your bob, Hannah?"

The little girl nodded enthusiastically, so Rose brushed her long hair, then had Hannah lay her head on the table the way Rose had done as a girl. It had been years since she'd done AnaMary's hair, and Rose struggled to roll the hair on each side of Hannah's head. It looked a little loose, but Rose fashioned the rest of her hair into a bun. She was putting pins in the bob to hold it in place when Martha entered the kitchen, cooing to the baby.

She put a pot of water on the stove, filled a bottle, and put it on to heat. Then she turned and noticed Hannah's bob. Her lips pursed. "I suppose it's been a while since you've done bobs."

Rose was pleasantly surprised that Martha's response, although critical, had been delivered in a civil matter. Maybe David's quiet censuring had brought about the change.

"I can hold the baby while you fix Hannah's hair." Rose rounded the table to where Martha was heating the bottle.

"No, that's all right. He can go in the cradle for a few minutes." Martha crossed the kitchen to place Amos in the wooden cradle in the dining room.

As soon as she sat him down, Amos squalled. The sound made Rose want to snatch him up and cuddle him, but Martha seemed determined to keep Rose away from the baby. While Martha was occupied undoing Hannah's bob, Rose slipped into the dining room. She wouldn't defy Martha and pick up Amos, but she tapped a foot against the rocker to tip the cradle slightly, and then she let it go. Soon she'd developed a rhythm that rocked the cradle, and Amos quieted.

Ignoring Hannah's whines and protests, Martha rebrushed the small girl's hair, and then, after twisting strands on each side of Hannah's head into crisp, smooth rolls, she drew the hair back and into a tight bun.

Rose longed to comfort the little girl who was missing her Daed and Mamm. She wondered how long Esther would be away and where she'd gone. Hannah had started to say, but Martha cut her off. Was she caring for ill relatives or maybe in the hospital? Wherever their mother was, she hoped Esther would return soon. Martha seemed to need a break from childcare.

The day was filled with chores, but Martha refused Rose's help. She spent time teaching the girls, and although she was a little critical of the results, for the most part, she was patient with both of them. Whenever Rose ended up in a room alone with one of the children, Martha charged in and snatched the child.

In the midafternoon, Martha put all three children down for their naps. Rose suggested Martha lie down for a while.

"I can listen for the girls while you rest."

"No thank you." Martha marched off to her bedroom to feed Amos a bottle.

A short while later, Rose heard snores coming from the room and peeked in to see Martha asleep with baby Amos beside her. She tiptoed into the room, picked up the baby, fed him the rest of his bottle, and tucked him into the crib. Then she went upstairs to listen for the girls.

Hannah woke first, and Rose read stories with her until Martha shuffled out of the room downstairs. Rose whispered to Hannah that she was going to her room, and the small girl looked as if she understood. By the time Martha climbed the stairs, Rose was sitting in the back bedroom, reading a nursing magazine she'd brought from home.

The nap must have refreshed Martha because she read a few books with the girls and even laughed and joked with them a little. Rose had been wondering why Jonathan had chosen such a grouchy caretaker for his children, but maybe Martha was only tired.

"Time to start dinner," Martha announced, and Hannah danced out of the room and downstairs, singing.

Rose debated about following them downstairs or finishing her magazine. If she volunteered to help, Martha would refuse. Still it would be impolite not to ask, so Rose went to the kitchen.

Some of the tiredness around Martha's eyes and mouth had eased, and she appeared almost cheerful. When she spotted Rose, though, her face tightened. Although she waved away Rose's offers of assistance, she had Hannah and Libby stand beside her as she chopped and cooked. Martha seemed to enjoy teaching the girls, and Rose wondered why David and Martha had no children of their own. Perhaps they hadn't been married long.

After the chicken potpie was bubbling on the stove, Martha removed the dough for the potpie squares from the gas-powered refrigerator and showed the girls how to roll it out. They took turns, and both were covered in flour by the time they were done cutting the squares. Martha only smiled and brushed them off.

"Your Daed will be pleased that you helped with dinner tonight," she told them.

Hannah clapped and sang, "Daed's coming, Daed's coming."

Libby followed her around repeating the word *Daed*.

Rose smiled at their antics, but she understood their excitement. Her own heart was singing because she'd soon be seeing Jonathan. She had to keep reminding herself he was off-limits.

The minute he walked through the door, though, she forgot all her internal warnings. Her pulse went into overdrive, and she had to tear her gaze away before he noticed her staring. Seeing him made her wish she were Amish again, but even if she were, he belonged to another woman.

As soon as Hannah had greeted him with a hug, she took her Daed's hand and dragged him through the living room. "I made potpie."

"You helped," Martha corrected from the kitchen.

Once again Rose was struck by the differences in Englisch and Amish child-rearing. An Englisch mother would praise her child for an accomplishment like that, but the Amish considered it Hochmut. They didn't want their children to become prideful. She was torn over which was best, but watching Hannah deflate, Rose leaned more toward the Englisch ways.

When Hannah passed her, Rose whispered so Martha couldn't hear, "You did a good job with dinner." She hoped she wasn't undermining Martha's child-rearing by offering Hannah some encouragement.

Hannah beamed and the skip returned to her step. Jonathan caught Rose's eye and mouthed, "Thank you." That lit up her world, the same way she'd lit up Hannah's. Hochmut or not, she was thrilled.

8

Jonathan's spirits had risen when he pulled into his brother's driveway. For the first time in a long time, he'd finished the milking early enough that he could have dinner with his family. He tried not to think he'd been motivated to get done early so he could see Rose, but his conscience nagged at him.

It bothered him even more when she was standing in the living room with Hannah to greet him. He forced himself to concentrate on Hannah's chatter when every fiber of his being was drawn toward Rose. He swept Hannah into his arms for a hug, wishing he could do the same with Rose.

If she'd dressed in Englisch clothes, it might have been easier to keep his mind off her. Or maybe not. Englisch clothes at least would remind him not to be foolish.

He stepped through the kitchen doorway, conscious she was close behind him, but Libby's welcoming smile drew him around the table. Hannah stood beside him, leaning into him, while he knelt and hugged Libby. Being with the two of them eased some of the relentless sadness and loneliness of his days and made him more determined to spend more time with them. He needed to find a way to keep them with him, but how?

"We weren't expecting you this early." Martha bustled over to the table with another place setting. "But we're happy you're here," she amended. "Have a seat."

Jonathan sat on the bench beside Libby and was delighted to discover Rose sitting opposite him with Hannah by her side. He indulged in a brief fantasy that they were a family, having dinner together. Except if they were a family, he'd be at the head of the table with Rose to his left. Picturing how he'd reach under the table and take her hand made him smile until he realized Rose had her head tilted and a questioning look on her face. He'd been staring at her this whole time. His face heated, and his grin disappeared.

He shook his head to dislodge the fantasies. "I'm sorry," he said to Rose. "I was lost in thought." *About you.* Jonathan was grateful his back was to Martha. If she'd seen him gawking at Rose like that, she'd have given him a lecture. Although maybe that's what he needed—one of Martha's scoldings to remind him to rein in his fantasies.

He forced his thoughts away from Rose. "Is Amos still sleeping?"

Martha glanced at the clock. "He didn't go down for his nap until thirty minutes ago, so he'll likely sleep through dinner."

The back door opened, and David entered the kitchen. He stopped and stared at Jonathan. "What brings you here so early?"

"I missed the children." Jonathan hoped that didn't sound like a lame excuse. He'd missed them before, but he hadn't managed to finish his chores in time.

His brother's raised eyebrows indicated he had some doubts about the excuse. David glanced at Rose, and Jonathan's stomach clenched the way it had when they were younger whenever Rose and his brother were together. He examined David's face for some sign of feelings for Rose, but his brother's face remained expressionless. Relief flooded through Jonathan before he remembered that they were no longer teens in competition for the same girl.

"Nice to see you at the meal." David clapped him on the back in passing.

After they were all seated around the table and the prayer had been said, conversation grew stilted. David tried to engage Jonathan in talk about some milking difficulties, but Jonathan couldn't form coherent thoughts on the topics with Rose sitting directly across from him. Somehow, milking, which usually consumed much of his thoughts, paled in comparison with Rose.

Martha fastened her gaze on him. "So how are the vegetables coming along?"

"Fine, fine." Her reminder about the garden made Jonathan cringe inside. He'd hoped to delay taking Rose to town. He wanted to have more time with her. Would it be dishonest to hide the fact that he had deliveries tomorrow?

Before he could decide, Martha asked, "When will you be doing your next delivery?"

Jonathan couldn't lie. "Tomorrow," he mumbled. Then he looked at Rose. "When I do my deliveries, I can take you to the station."

"Thank you. I'd appreciate it."

Was it his imagination, or did she look as disappointed as he felt? Hannah danced over to him. "Can I go too?"

Martha cleared her throat. "I—"

Jonathan rushed to answer before Martha told her *no*. "Yes, Hannah you may." He didn't want a repeat of other nights, when he'd felt obligated to uphold Martha's rules.

His daughter stared at him starry-eyed. "I can?"

Martha pursed her lips and crossed her arms. "I'm not so sure that's a good idea. What will she do when you go into the restaurants?"

"She'll come with me." He turned to his daughter. "You'd like that, wouldn't you, Hannah?"

Hannah beamed and nodded.

Martha shook her head. "You'll have your arms filled with crates. How can you hold her hand? What if she dashes out into the street?"

"I could go along to keep an eye on her," Rose offered. "I don't mind taking a later train."

Sucking in a breath, Martha pinned Jonathan with a steely glare. "She needs someone reliable to watch her. Might be better for her to stay here."

Jonathan understood she didn't trust Rose, but he couldn't believe she'd just insulted Rose like that. He shot Martha a warning glance. Her arguments against taking Hannah along also made him aware of how much Martha had taken charge of all the decisions about his children. He hoped they wouldn't get into a battle of wills over every decision he made, now that he planned to assert himself.

Hannah glanced from one to the other, her hands clasped in front of her anxiously. Jonathan wanted to reassure her. He'd need to talk privately with Martha about this. Arguing in front of the children wasn't good for them.

He beckoned to Hannah, and when she came to him, he lifted her onto his lap. "I said you could go, and you may." Then he turned to Rose. "I don't want you to miss your train. Hannah and I will be fine."

"Probably safer," Martha muttered, but she subsided when he looked directly at her.

"I like Rose," Hannah said. "Can she come too?"

Hugging Hannah to him, Jonathan wished Rose could spend the whole time with them. "She'll ride with us to town. After that, we'll see about her schedule."

Martha picked up the serving dishes and turned her back to the table, but if the stiffness of her shoulders was any indication, she was fuming.

Rose stood and reached for some of the dishes. "Is there anything I can do to help?"

"No." Martha said gruffly.

Rose lowered her hands to her sides. Her eager expression changed to a neutral one, but hurt flickered in her eyes.

Jonathan ached inside for her. Although he'd always admired Martha's bluntness and honesty, he wished for Rose's sake that his sister-in-law would be kind. He shifted Hannah in his arms, pushed back the bench, and stood. "I'm going to put all the children to bed tonight."

"But, but—" Martha sounded as if she were gasping for air.

Jonathan expected a protest, so he spoke firmly. "I didn't get to see them last night. Since you don't need Rose's help down here, she could help me get the children ready for bed. If she'd like to, that is." Jonathan's heart warmed at Rose's grateful glance.

Martha turned from the sink. "I don't think that's—"

Jonathan cut her off before she could hurt Rose's feelings again. "I'll be fine. You deserve some time off." He stood, and Hannah wound her arms around his neck. "I'll carry her up." He caught Rose's eye and motioned toward Libby, who was nodding off at the table. "Could you get Libby?"

Rose's smile took his breath away. "I'd be happy to." She lifted Libby into her arms. Her eyes heavy, the little girl snuggled against Rose.

Martha hissed out a breath between her teeth. Jonathan almost did the same, but for a totally different reason. Seeing Rose cuddling his daughter did strange things to his insides. Maybe Martha was right. This wasn't a good idea.

Rose loved the feel of the little girls' arms around her neck as they each hugged her good night. Watching them hug their Daed brought tears to her eyes. When she tucked Hannah under the covers, the small girl begged for a story. Rose sent a questioning glance to Jonathan.

"Only one. We still need to feed Amos. He hasn't eaten yet." He settled at the foot of Libby's bed.

His presence there and being a part of bedtime rituals stirred the earlier longing to have a family of her own. If only these were her children and Jonathan were her husband and they were putting their girls to bed. Rose's heart swelled at the idea. After they tucked the children in bed, he'd take her hand and . . .

Hannah tugged at her arm, interrupting her daydream. "This one?"

Rose took the book she held out, opened the cover, and began reading. She turned the book so Libby could see the pictures, even though Libby's eyes kept fluttering closed. Each time Libby started to doze off Rose sneaked a peek at Jonathan.

When she closed the book, Rose stole one more glance. Although his gaze rested on her, he seemed lost in dreamland. Was he picturing Esther instead? The thought pained her.

After the girls received one more hug and kiss from each of them, Rose and Jonathan went downstairs to find David in the living room holding Amos while Martha warmed his bottle.

Rose thought her heart couldn't get any fuller, but when Jonathan bent and took Amos from his brother, her chest ached. As he stood there cradling his son, the love in his eyes overwhelmed her. She had to turn her head away to hide her misty eyes. Esther was a lucky woman.

"Would you like to hold him while I get his bottle?" Jonathan asked.

Rose blinked to clear her eyes before she faced him. "Me?"

Jonathan's gentle smile warmed her from head to toe. "Yes, you."

David cleared his throat. "I don't think . . ." He got to his feet and walked toward them.

Jonathan ignored him and brought Amos over to her. Their eyes met, and Rose was drowning in his brown eyes. His arms brushed hers as he held the baby out. If she'd already been holding Amos, she might have dropped him. She only prayed Jonathan wasn't close enough to hear the rapid thumping of her heart.

Taking a deep breath to steady herself, Rose reached for Amos.

A loud screech behind her made her jump and startled Amos, who wailed loudly. Martha came up behind Rose and snatched Amos from her arms.

"You almost dropped him." Martha's chest was heaving, and Rose worried she might hyperventilate again. "And listen to him crying." She patted Amos on the back. "There, there. It's all right," she said between rapid breaths.

Rose longed to point out the crying and the near fall had been the result of Martha startling them. Once again, Martha had put Rose on the defensive. Jonathan shot Rose an apologetic glance.

Then he stepped over to Martha. "Thank you for the rescue, but I'm not sure it would have been necessary if you hadn't screamed."

"You're blaming me?" Martha's indignant tone indicated she didn't feel she deserved his criticism. "You would have screamed too, if you'd seen what I saw. If I hadn't intervened, Amos would have fallen on his head."

"In that case, thank you for your swift action."

Martha appeared mollified by Jonathan's acknowledgment. "You're welcome. I love Amos and don't want anything to happen to him."

"I know you do, and I appreciate how well you care for him." He reached for his son. "Is the bottle ready? I'm going to change him before I feed him."

"I already changed him while you were upstairs, and the bottle's ready, but I'd be happy to feed Amos. You've had a long day and must be tired." Martha turned slightly, making it hard for Jonathan to reach the baby.

Rose wondered if they'd engage in a tug of war, and she was reminded of Solomon judging the two mothers. Which one was the real parent? Martha seemed to be asserting her claim, but Rose suspected her love ran deep enough to give up the baby, if it meant saving his life.

Once again, Jonathan held out his arms. "Thank you for everything you've done. I'm sure you must be even more tired than I am, so I'll take care of feeding Amos tonight."

Martha looked as if she might not surrender the baby until David said her name softly. With her jaw set in mutinous lines, she handed over the baby. "I'll go get the bottle, but hold him tight." She sent a warning glance in Rose's direction.

After Martha entered the kitchen, David said in a low voice, "You have to understand how attached she's become to the children. She cares about them deeply."

"I do understand," Jonathan said, "but—" He stopped speaking when Martha entered with the bottle.

"Why don't you sit on the couch?" she suggested.

Jonathan sank onto the couch and accepted the bottle from her. With his chin, he motioned for Rose to sit beside him. Before she could cross the room, Martha plopped down beside Jonathan, so close they almost bumped elbows. Then she tried to attract David's attention, but he was staring at Rose with sympathy.

Martha's lips pinched together, and she looked like she might cry. Rose gestured toward his wife, and David reddened. As soon as Martha caught his eye, she gave a quick toss of her head to indicate he should sit on the other side of Jonathan. With an apologetic glance at Rose, David trudged to the couch and sat where Martha had indicated.

Rose stood awkwardly in the center of the room, closed out of the family gathering. An outsider. Was this her payback for leaving the Amish?

Jonathan had been unsuccessfully trying to wrest the bottle from Martha's grasp. When David sat beside him, he felt hemmed in—not only by Martha and David but by Martha's determination to care for Amos.

Across the room from him, Rose appeared isolated and lonely. That same feeling haunted him day and night. He wanted to reach out to her, draw her close. *Of course, the only reason you want to hold her is to comfort her.* Once again, his conscience jabbed him. He was still in mourning and shouldn't be thinking that way about Rose or any woman. Especially not an *Englischer.*

But she was also a guest, one they'd shut out. Jonathan stood and, cradling Amos in one arm, held out a hand. "Thanks for the bottle, Martha."

Reluctantly, she released it, and Jonathan headed toward Rose. As much as he wanted to feed his son, he wanted to make up for their treatment of Rose.

"Would you like to feed Amos?"

He barely heard Martha's gasp because a beautiful smile lit Rose's face, and the room around him faded. Nothing—no one—existed except for the two of them. The sensation lasted only a second before Jonathan shook himself. His back was to Martha and David. Had they seen? And most of all, had Rose noticed?

He struggled to regain his composure. To act normal. Instead of walking toward Rose, he veered toward the rocking chair. "Maybe, um, maybe you might be more comfortable here."

She followed him and sat where he'd indicated. When she held out her arms, she looked as if he were giving her a precious gift. *She must love babies.*

Behind him, Martha made choking noises as he lowered Amos into Rose's arms, but Jonathan remained fully focused on his son and

Rose. As he settled his son into her arms, he brushed the softness of her skin, and he swallowed hard. Rose seemed unaffected as she cuddled Amos close and nuzzled his cheek. When he handed her the bottle, she touched it to Amos's lips lightly several times until he opened his mouth. Her expertise surprised him, but it shouldn't have. *She must have fed many babies at the hospital.*

At seeing the two of them together, an ache started in his chest and spread through him. Rose mothering his son brought up all his grief at losing Esther. His eyes blurred with tears, and he forced himself to turn away.

There, he faced a different sight. Martha's eyes, wide and worried, were fixed on Rose with the glittering intensity of a crow on a worm. David had an arm around her, but Jonathan couldn't be sure whether it was for comfort or to restrain Martha.

Jonathan's guilt over Martha's suffering prompted him to return to the rocker. "Would it be all right if I held him?"

Rose looked up at him and blinked several times as if he'd startled her out of a daydream. "What? Oh, of course." She started to get up, but he set a hand on her shoulder.

"No need to move. I'll just take him over there." He waved toward the armchair near the sofa.

With practiced movements, Rose lifted Amos, keeping one hand on the bottle. When she settled Amos into his outstretched arms, a look of sadness crossed her face, and he wished he hadn't taken the baby from her.

9

Sadness enveloped Rose as she climbed the stairs a short while later. Holding Amos had opened a hole inside her that would never be filled. Each time she held someone else's child, she longed for a baby of her own. Being around Jonathan only added to her sorrow. Years ago, she'd fled to escape the pain of him marrying Esther. Back then she'd been a teen with a crush on an older boy. That boy had turned into a man who haunted her dreams.

Tomorrow she'd leave here forever. She'd never be back. Though the pull to return was strong, she had no reason to. Her family had rejected her, and the only man she'd ever loved was married.

A few tears slipped down her cheeks and wet her pillow. Rose dashed them away with a finger. Perhaps Martha was right. Crying was a waste of time. Rose needed to focus on the positives in life. She had a job, an apartment, friends, and her health. She'd chosen a profession she loved. Nursing kept her too busy to think, to reminisce, and to indulge in her sorrow. And for that, she was grateful.

She'd almost drifted off when tiny feet padded down the hallway to her room. Her door creaked open, and Hannah peeked inside. Martha's words echoed in her ear, but when Hannah sniffled, Rose sat up and spread her arms wide. Hannah raced to her, and Rose hugged her close.

Hannah's chest heaved with silent sobs, and Rose wondered how many nights the little girl lay in bed, crying soundlessly.

Stroking Hannah's hair, she whispered, "What's the matter, sweetie?"

"I miss Mamm." Hannah's voice was thick with tears.

"I'm so sorry." Rose wished she knew more about the situation so she could offer comfort. If Esther wouldn't be gone long, Rose could reassure Hannah her Mamm would be back soon. Although Rose was tempted to ask, Martha had been adamant about not bringing it up. No sense in breaking another rule. She'd already broken Martha's rule about putting Hannah back in her own bed. She'd couldn't bear to think of Hannah crying alone in her bed. Holding Hannah eased some of Rose's sorrow. Both of them needed comfort tonight.

Rose had intended to carry Hannah back to her bed as soon as she fell asleep, but just before dawn, Amos's cries woke her. Had he cried at all during the night? If he had, Rose hadn't heard him. If he'd slept through the night, Rose wondered if it was because Jonathan had fed him and put him down for the night.

While Martha tended to Amos, Rose gathered Hannah in her arms, carried her down the hall, and lowered her into bed. Hannah's arms snaked around Rose's neck and, though she wanted to stay there, she didn't want to face Martha's wrath. She gently disentangled herself from Hannah's grip and tucked her under the covers. Then she slipped down the hall to get ready for the day ahead.

She was dressed and ready when Martha came up to wake the girls.

Martha's eyebrows rose. "You're up early today. You must be excited about getting back to New York."

Rose wasn't sure how to respond. In one way, she'd be glad to leave, but another part of her was reluctant. Because she couldn't explain that to Martha, she ended up shrugging. This time she didn't offer to help, although it made her feel guilty to see Martha do all work. Once the girls were dressed, Martha hustled them downstairs for breakfast.

Martha set a few pieces of cereal in front of Amos. He picked them up in his chubby fist and ate them one by one while she placed bowls of oatmeal in front of everyone else. She set maple syrup and applesauce on the table, adding a dollop of each to the girls' bowls. Rose added some to hers and stirred it around. It had been a long time since she'd had her oatmeal the Amish way, and she'd missed it.

She'd miss a lot of things when she left today.

She was disappointed Jonathan didn't show up for breakfast, but she'd be seeing him later that day. Hannah twirled around the table singing at the top of her lungs, "Daed is coming," and Rose wanted to join her.

Martha didn't scold Hannah until the two of them collided and Martha nearly dropped the dishes she was carrying. A few minutes later, Martha hummed as she washed the dishes. She seemed to be in a good mood this morning. Was it because she'd had a good night's sleep or because she was happy Rose was leaving? Either way, it was a pleasant change.

By the time Jonathan arrived, Rose was antsy. Martha kept the girls busy with chores, but Rose had little to do except daydream and review every moment—past and recent—she'd spent with Jonathan. Eating lunch had provided the only distraction.

As soon as Jonathan's wagon pulled into the driveway, Martha rushed to the door to greet Jonathan. "Did you have lunch?"

"I'm in a hurry." Jonathan hefted Rose's suitcase to take it out to the wagon.

"I assume that means no." Martha hurried into the kitchen and returned with two sandwiches and an apple. She tucked them into a plastic bag. "You can eat that while you're on the road." She looked at Rose and shook her head. "He'd forget to eat if I didn't keep after him."

Rose was surprised by Martha's sudden camaraderie. Her pleasant mood seemed to extend even to their conversations. Or should she say, *conversation*. That was the only thing Martha had said to her since early that morning.

Libby toddled over to her Daed and lifted her arms for a hug. Jonathan set down the suitcase and lunch bag, picked her up, and cuddled her. Libby rubbed her eyes, stuck her thumb in her mouth, and set her head on Jonathan's shoulder. Rose tucked that picture into her memory for later daydreams.

Martha hurried over. "It's nap time." She reached for Libby, who seemed reluctant to let her Daed go. Martha untangled Libby's arm from around Jonathan's neck and, lips pinched together, he handed her over to Martha.

"Actually," Martha said, "Hannah should have her nap too. Why don't I take them both upstairs now so you can leave?"

Hannah burst into tears. "I want to go with Daed."

Jonathan put a hand on her head. "Shh, Hannah. You're going with me. Let's not wake Amos."

Her mouth open in midcry, Hannah studied his face as if to be sure he was telling the truth. Then she released a long sigh and leaned against him.

"What about her nap?" Martha seemed determined to have her way.

Jonathan only shrugged. "If she's sleepy, she can nap in the wagon. I'm sure she'll be fine. Please don't worry."

"I do worry about them. All the time. Speaking of that, could I speak to you privately in the kitchen for a minute?" Martha sounded almost frantic.

"Can it wait? I really need to get on the road."

"No, it's urgent." Martha tugged at his arm.

Jonathan's lips thinned into a straight line, and he followed Martha into the kitchen. Rose tuned out the whispered conversation until her name was mentioned.

"Promise me you won't let Rose watch Hannah. Please, Jonathan."

"Look, Martha, I've told you twice already, we'll most likely be dropping Rose off at the station first. Although if we don't get out the door soon, she may have to ride along to the deliveries."

"I'll let you go now, so you can get her to the train, but hearing you say 'most likely' makes me nervous. You know how irresponsible she is."

Jonathan emerged from the kitchen with Martha close on his tail. "Please don't worry," he said. "I'll take good care of Hannah. I wouldn't want anything to happen to my daughter."

Behind him, Martha winced when he said the last two words, and her arms tightened around Libby. "Please remember what I said."

Jonathan strode across the room, picked up Hannah, and lifted the suitcase. "Thank you for your advice. I'll be very careful."

Rose scurried over and grabbed the lunch bag before Jonathan left it behind. She'd left a thank-you note on the bed in Martha's back bedroom along with a small gift she'd brought to give her sister, but she wanted to let Martha know she appreciated the roof over her head. "Danke for having me. I—"

Martha cut her off and tried one more time to convince Jonathan as they walked out the door. "The safest place for Hannah is in bed for a nap." After Jonathan sat Hannah on the middle of the wagon seat between him and Rose, she called out, "I'll be praying."

Rose mulled over the words Martha had said in the kitchen. *She called me irresponsible.* What had given her that idea?

Jonathan smiled over at Rose after he'd turned onto the main road. "It's a lovely day for a ride, jah?"

Any day was a lovely day if she was riding with him. As Rose returned his smile, she let go of all the tension she'd been under at Martha's and relaxed into the pleasure of sitting beside Hannah and Jonathan.

Beside her, Hannah chattered away, pointing out birds, flowers, clouds, and other horses. She waved to every car and buggy that passed. Rose hadn't noticed this chatty side of her at Martha's house and wondered if she'd been as constrained there as Rose had.

Rose enjoyed her comments and asked questions to keep the conversation going. Jonathan's eyes crinkled, and he smiled at her over Hannah's head.

"Our Hannah loves to talk, don't you?" Jonathan put an arm around his daughter and gave her a quick hug before returning his hand to the reins. "Not everyone appreciates her steady flow, so it's nice for her to be around someone who likes it. Even if you're only being polite."

"Not at all. It's a pleasure." Or it had been until Jonathan used the word *our*, reminding Rose of his marriage. Her spirits sank, but it was hard to stay gloomy with such upbeat company. Rose pushed her disappointment aside to concentrate on Hannah, although she still got sidetracked when she glanced toward the driver's side of the wagon, which she did quite often. Strong tanned hands guiding the horse, broad shoulders, sparkling eyes that took her breath away rekindled memories of him.

Hannah interrupted her reverie. "Daed lets me help in the barn with milking."

Rose smiled at her. "I bet you're a big help."

"I am, but not as much help as Mamm." Her lips drooped.

"It's all right, Hannah. I don't expect you to take Mamm's place." Jonathan gave her another brief squeeze.

Her chin quivering, Hannah turned to Rose. "Mamm's in heaven." Her eyes filled with tears. "Forever and ever."

Rose drew in a sharp breath and glanced over at Jonathan to be sure it was true before she responded. Jonathan, his lips pressed tightly together, stared off into the distance, but his terse nod confirmed Hannah's statement.

Slipping her arm around Hannah, Rose drew her close. "I'm so sorry," she said to both of them.

They rode in silence for a while, and Hannah's eyes fluttered open and shut several times before she fell sleep.

Rose wanted to ask Jonathan about his wife, but his profile appeared so forbidding. It was as if he'd shuttered all his feelings behind a stiff and stoic mask. "I'm sorry," she said again, but the words seemed so inadequate. "I didn't know."

With a bleak look on his face, Jonathan gave a brief nod and didn't speak as they passed the next two farms. Then he said, "The past eight months have been difficult."

"Eight months? Amos?"

"Yes, Esther died during childbirth. I couldn't have gotten through this long without Martha."

Rose reevaluated her negative opinion of Martha. No wonder she was overprotective, and she must be exhausted after caring for a baby and two other little ones. "So all the children stay with her?"

"We've been flip-flopping back and forth. Sometimes they're with me, other times with Martha." He switched the reins to his other hand and rubbed his forehead. "Martha wants to keep them full time."

Martha did seem to act as if they were her own children. That also explained some of the tension between her and Jonathan over Hannah's naptime and the bedtime routine last night. "She wants to keep them for good?"

"She says until I marry again, but I don't know if I can ever marry again. Losing someone you love is too painful."

Rose understood that, but most widows and widowers in the Amish community remarried sometime after their one-year mourning period ended. Perhaps Jonathan would too. Although it was hard for Rose to think about him marrying someone else, she wanted to make him feel better. "You may change your mind after you're done grieving."

Jonathan shook his head. "No, I don't want to go through the heartache again."

Although he was only an arm's length away, he'd moved to a place so far from her that she couldn't reach him or comfort him.

10

Rose's stomach clenched as they headed past a neighboring farm. Her childhood home was next.

She sucked in a breath.

"Is everything all right?" Jonathan stared at her with concern.

"Y-yes. It's just that . . ." Rose waved in the direction of her family's farm.

"Oh." He studied her face. "You're probably hurting as much as I am."

Rose's loss couldn't compare with his. "I haven't been through a death like you have."

"Isn't a broken relationship like a death?" Jonathan mused. "Maybe it's even harder, because when a person dies, you know they didn't have a choice. But when a relationship ends, they did."

"That's true." Rose had never thought if it like that, but her Daed's rejection had cut her off from her family for good. She couldn't blame the severed relationship on her father. "In my case, I caused that rejection by my actions. If I hadn't run away from home . . ."

"If only we could go back and erase past mistakes."

Rose wasn't sure she'd do anything differently if she could return to the day she'd decided to run away. Back then, she'd needed to get away from Daed's cruelty and from Jonathan's marriage.

They'd reached the house, and Rose spied a flash of blue in the garden. "AnaMary!" Her sister was weeding the vegetables, a job they used to do together.

Jonathan slowed the wagon. "Do you want to stop?"

There was nothing Rose wanted more. "I can't make you late for your deliveries."

"What's more important? Family or timely deliveries?" Jonathan pulled the wagon to the side of the road. "If there's one thing I learned these past eight months, it's to spend as much time as you can with the people you love. You never know how long you'll have them." He leaned over, eased Hannah away from her side, and sat with his sleeping daughter on the seat.

"Thank you." Rose flashed him a grateful smile and flew from the wagon. Daed's bedroom was on the other side of the house, so he wouldn't see her talking to AnaMary. She didn't call out her sister's name as she raced across the yard, but AnaMary glanced up and saw her coming.

Her mouth open, AnaMary jumped to her feet and brushed off her hands. She glanced fearfully toward the house, but she overcame her skittishness to give Rose a long, hard hug. "I've missed you so much," she said with tears in her eyes. "Tell me what you're doing now."

Rose condensed the story of the long, lonely years away from home. The strangeness of living in the Englisch world, the hardships, and the endless hours of studying and learning. She tried to highlight the worst of it to prevent her sister from doing what she had done.

"I'd love to run away," AnaMary burst out, her fists knotted. "I don't care how hard it is. I hate it here." Tears spurted from her eyes.

"I felt the same way, so I understand."

"No, you don't. You have no idea." AnaMary wrung her hands. "I can't stand around talking. I need to get some weeding done."

"Let me help." Rose knelt in the garden, breathing in the scent of the rich earth, the tomatoey smell of the nearby leaves, so different from the hot, tarry asphalt, the acres of cement, and buildings so tall they blocked the sun. "I can't stay long, but I'll at least do one row while you tell me."

Living in the city, Rose had missed the green. Here the tomato plants stood tall and green against their wooden stakes, and plump red tomatoes hung heavy on the branches. Bean plants wound their way up the poles, with green beans dangling among the leaves. In the distance fields of cornstalks reached to the sky.

AnaMary knelt in a different row and began yanking weeds fast and furiously. Rose used her discarded spade to dig out the more deeply rooted ones.

Her sister's story poured out along with her tears. "When you were here, we did chores together, but now I have to do yours and mine, plus Daed's and Mamm's, because Mamm has arthritis. I also have to take care of Daed, who refuses to listen to the doctor's orders, and he doesn't listen to anything I say. I'd hoped you . . ." AnaMary burst into a fresh spate of tears.

"Oh, AnaMary, I'm so sorry." Rose wanted to hug her sister, but helping her with the work would be more productive. "If only there were something I could do."

AnaMary's litany continued. "I can't court anyone; I have no time. Mamm and Daed need a *Daadihaus*, and I need a husband who can help with the work—the mowing and farming chores, milking the cows. Whatever I don't get done, Daed tries to do. You know how he is."

Yes, Rose knew exactly how stubborn and determined he could be. She nodded and moved down the row.

"I'd run away in an instant, but how can I leave them without help? All I dream about day and night is escaping."

Rose had never considered how running away would affect her sister. She felt guilty for complaining earlier about her difficult schoolwork and rough adjustment to the Englisch world. AnaMary had been struggling under burdens the two of them should have shared. If she'd stayed here, she would have married David, and Daed would have had someone to help with the outdoor work. AnaMary could have courted someone and married by now. Instead, she was left with an endless round of chores.

"I wish I could think of a way to help you." Rose couldn't go back to New York and leave AnaMary stranded here. Even if she could afford to pay for outside help, her parents never would accept it. People in the Amish community helped each other, though. "Have you tried talking to the bishop?"

"Daed would kill me if I told anyone we need help. He's determined to do it all himself without any help, even if it kills him. Which it might."

A loud shout came from the front yard. "Stop it! Let go!"

AnaMary's eyes bulged. "That's Daed. What's he doing out of bed?"

Rose and AnaMary raced around to the front of the house to find Jonathan trying to wrestle the push mower from Daed.

"Aren't you supposed to be in bed?" Jonathan kept a firm grip on the handle. "You're not going to take a chance on mowing the lawn. I'll mow it for you."

"Let go of the mower right now." Red-faced and panting, Daed yanked on the mower. "You have no right to stop me."

"Please," Jonathan said, "think about your heart. What did the doctors say?"

"They don't know anything. A little exercise never hurt anyone." Sweat rolled down Daed's cheeks.

"Daed!" Rose yelled "Stop it. You'll have another heart attack. Jonathan's right. You belong in bed."

Her father turned toward her. "What are you doing here? I told you never to come to this house again." Spotting AnaMary behind her, he shook his finger at her. "You went behind my back and contacted your sister."

Jonathan stepped in front of Rose and AnaMary. "Eli, please, calm down. What would God want you to do?"

"Move out of my way right now." Daed grabbed Jonathan's shoulder and tried to push him aside. When Jonathan didn't budge, Daed stood on tiptoe to scream at Rose. Pointing at her, he exploded, "This is all your fault! You . . . you . . ." He clutched at his chest and collapsed.

Rose raced around Jonathan and dropped to her knees beside Daed and tapped on his collarbone. He was unresponsive. "AnaMary, call 911. The phone in that shanty doesn't work."

AnaMary stood there close to tears.

Jonathan touched AnaMary's shoulder. "Stay there with your Daed." He ran for the wagon. "I'll call. The nearest neighbor with a phone is right down the road." That would be faster than running through the woods to his shop.

Rose put one hand on top of the other, interlocking her fingers, and pressed on his sternum. After each compression, she waited until his chest recoiled, and then pressed again. *Three, four, five . . .* Rose counted until she reached thirty.

Then she slid her hand under his neck to tilt his head back and open his airway. Pinching his nose, she completed two breaths and returned to thirty compressions. Like a machine, she repeated the rhythm over and over. Two breaths, thirty compressions, two breaths, thirty compressions . . . *Please, Daed, breathe.*

AnaMary stood over her, shaking. "Will he be all right?"

Rose had no time to answer her. She needed to keep an accurate count and to save her breath. The *two-thirty-two* pattern beat through her brain and traveled through her hands as she pounded on Daed's chest.

Jonathan pulled the wagon all the way into the driveway and tied up his horse. Then he dashed across the lawn. "They're on their way." He stayed a good distance away, giving her room. "Is there anything I can do?"

Rose couldn't interrupt her rhythm, but she managed to shake her head as she pounded on Daed's chest again.

Jonathan called to AnaMary, and she started. "Why don't you go call your Mamm? She'll probably want to ride in the ambulance with him."

AnaMary did as he suggested, which relieved Rose of that sense of something hovering overhead. *Thank you, Jonathan.*

When AnaMary returned, he called her over. "Maybe we could pray."

"Good idea," AnaMary said.

Rose was exhausted. Sweat slid down her forehead and burned her eyes. She closed them, trying to blink away the sting. Her hands ached. Her lungs hurt. The faint *weerow-weerow* of a siren in the distance gave her renewed energy. They'd be here soon. *Thirty-two-thirty.*

The siren grew louder. And then it pulled right out front. Doors banged open, and an EMT moved Rose aside and took over.

Rose rocked back on her heels. She wanted to collapse on the ground, but she had to get out of the way as the flurry of activity swirled around her. She stood and stumbled some distance away. AnaMary raced over and clung to Rose. Mamm supported herself by holding on to the doorjamb.

Her own arms still shaking from the compressions, Rose gently removed her sister's hands from around her. "We need to help Mamm get out to the ambulance."

AnaMary accompanied her to the front door, and together they assisted Mamm down the steps and across the lawn to the ambulance. Mamm and AnaMary squeezed into the front seat. Rose would ride in the back with Daed once he was situated.

Please, God, help Daed breathe.

Rose glanced around as they were loading Daed into the ambulance. Where was Jonathan? He stood beside the wagon, his back to her, holding Hannah, who was wailing. Rose wanted to go to him to thank him, but the EMTs had loaded Daed into the ambulance. She needed to leave. She tried calling out a thank-you, but Jonathan didn't hear her over the siren. Her last glimpse was of him, cradling Hannah, his hands over his daughter's ears, before the back doors slammed shut and the ambulance went screaming off down the road.

11

If Rose hadn't been a nurse, all the equipment and activity in the back of the ambulance would have frightened her, but she understood what the EMTs were doing to save Daed's life. She sat beside her father, holding his hand and praying.

Seeing him lying there helpless, barely clinging to life, melted some of Rose's resentment. Rather than focusing on her own hurt, memories of all he did for her as a child came flooding back, overshadowing the negative times. He had kept a roof over their heads, had done all the farm chores with no sons to assist him, had shown them how to milk cows and work in the fields, had driven her to work at Zook's Fry Pies, and had taught her about God. As a rebellious teen, she'd never appreciated any of those things. She'd only focused on his strictness and his temper, never noticing all the ways he'd shown his love.

If he died, she'd never be able to tell him how sorry she was and how much she loved him. Yes, the old bitterness still bubbled underneath, but in those moments between life and death, priorities changed. Rose ached inside to think Daed might never know she cared about him.

Ever mindful of the EMTs monitoring and working, she leaned as close as she could to whisper, "I love you, Daed." She repeated the words as the ambulance raced down the roads. She had no idea if he could hear them over the screaming siren, the hum of machinery, the clanks and rattles as they went over bumps, and the rumble of the engine, but she said them over and over.

Shortly before they arrived at the hospital, Daed's eyes fluttered open, and he turned his head in her direction. Rose wanted to shrink back so he didn't see her. She didn't want him to become agitated. She'd already caused this heart attack. But in the small enclosed space, she could lean away less than a foot. His cloudy eyes fixed on her face, and he mumbled something Rose couldn't understand.

She hoped he wasn't telling her to leave, because they were stuck in the ambulance together until they reached the hospital. "What, Daed?"

His lips moved forming words, but with all the noise around them and between his gasps for air, she wasn't positive she heard him. He repeated one word twice, and the second time she was almost sure he'd said "love."

Rose's heart swelled. Had he forgiven her? Was he trying to tell her he loved her? If those were the last words he ever uttered, he'd given her a precious gift. Her eyes blurred with tears, Rose said, "I love you, Daed." *And I always will.*

His eyes closed before she finished, and Rose hoped he'd heard her. But joy flooded through her to know he'd tried to tell her he loved her. Never once when she was growing up had he ever said those words, so that made them even more special.

With a great effort, Daed opened his eyes one more time. When he glanced in her direction, he struggled to speak.

Rose squeezed his hand gently. "Save your strength. I heard you. You said, 'I love you.'" She could barely choke out the words around the lump blocking her throat.

He made a slight motion with his head. Was that a nod? Rose wanted to believe it was.

Then he moved his mouth again to say one word. One word that came out clearly. One word that cut Rose to the core. One word that shut her out. "Ana . . ."

Had he mistaken her for her sister? Or did he want her to convey his message of love to AnaMary? Either way, he hadn't intended the word *love* for her.

Jonathan kept Hannah's ears covered until the siren faded into the distance. He worried about Rose and her Daed, and he sent up a quick prayer for them as well as for her family. Right now, though, he needed to calm Hannah's hysterics. Seeing and hearing the ambulance brought back the trauma for both of them. The night the ambulance rushed Esther to the hospital, she never returned.

He stroked Hannah's hair and repeated over and over, "It's all right. You're safe. Daed has you."

Hannah only shook her head and cried harder. She pushed words out between sobs, but Jonathan couldn't decipher them. Finally, a few words became clear. "Rose . . . die!"

"Oh, Hannah, do you think Rose is going to die because she went in an ambulance?" When his daughter nodded, he cuddled her closer. "Rose isn't hurt. She's only riding with someone else who needs help." He almost said *her Daed*, but didn't want her to connect the word *Daed* with ambulances. She had enough to worry about without wondering if he'd die. If only he could erase the night eight months ago from their memories. And take away his daughter's fears.

After her crying decreased, Hannah started babbling. "Mamm go in ambulance. Mamm die. Mamm go away forever and ever. Rose go in ambulance. Rose die. Rose go away forever and ever."

"No, Hannah. Rose is fine. She'll need a ride home from the hospital, so we can go and pick her up after I'm done with my work.

Do you want to go and see Rose?"

Hannah clapped and shouted a resounding *"Yes!"*

"Then we'll go do my deliveries, and as soon as we're done, we'll find Rose."

He hoped that wouldn't be too difficult, because she wouldn't have a ride home, nor would AnaMary or her Mamm. He'd stop by and offer to take them. Hannah could see Rose and so could he. He'd also find out about her Daed's condition. How serious was his heart attack?

The scene kept running through Jonathan's mind. He'd been the cause of Eli's temper. If he hadn't tried to stop Eli from mowing the lawn . . . He'd only been trying to help, but instead he'd started a wrestling match and screaming bout. Seeing Rose only added to Eli's frustration. Perhaps if Jonathan hadn't upset Eli, he wouldn't have been as furious at Rose and he'd never have had a heart attack. A voice in the back of his head kept telling him he was to blame.

To keep Hannah's mind off her Mamm and the ambulance as well as her worries about Rose, Jonathan asked her if she wanted to help him drive the wagon. She was delighted to sit on his lap and help hold the reins. That kept her occupied until they arrived at the first restaurant. Jonathan wished Rose were with them to watch Hannah, but he explained to his daughter that she needed to stay near him at all times.

Hannah indicated she understood, but he was unprepared for her to wrap her arms around his leg and drag along behind. It made carrying crates into the restaurants more difficult and slowed him down, but at least Martha didn't have to worry about Hannah's safety while he was working. His usually extroverted daughter surprised him not only with her clinginess but also with her shyness. Whenever he introduced her to each restaurant owner or manager, she hid behind him. Maybe the ambulance had traumatized her more than he realized.

Each time they returned to the wagon, she announced, "Now we go to see Rose," no matter how many times he explained that they'd go after all the crates had been emptied. Hannah peered over the seat to count them, but she still asked the same question after each delivery: "Now?"

Once the last crate had been left at a restaurant, Jonathan clucked to the horse and moved out into traffic. This time when Hannah asked, "Now?" he could say yes. He had to keep an arm around her to prevent her from falling out in her exuberance.

They pulled up outside the hospital, and Jonathan tied the horse to a hitching post at the far side of the parking lot. Hannah skipped along beside him, singing, "We're going to see Rose." Jonathan hoped she wouldn't be disappointed.

Although she'd been blindsided, Rose stayed with Daed during the admissions process and then helped AnaMary support Mamm to a chair in the waiting room. Mamm appeared dazed, but she patted Rose's arm.

"It's so good to see you," she whispered. "I've missed you, but once your Daed's . . ."

Rose's chest constricted until it hurt to breathe. "I know, Mamm. Daed won't want to see me." He'd made that clear when she came to the house the other day, in the yard before his heart attack, and a short while ago in the ambulance.

"I'm so sorry. I've tried talking to him about it, but it only makes him angry."

"Thank you, but I understand." Rose leaned over and hugged her Mamm. "I've missed you too." When she set her hand back on the chair arm, Mamm rested her hand on top.

"Tell me about what you've been doing," Mamm said.

"Didn't you get my letters?"

Mamm looked puzzled. "No. Did you write?"

Daed must have confiscated the letters. After the first few months of confusion, Rose had figured out how to send mail at the post office. She'd written a letter every week for the first year, but when she received no replies, the frequency had dwindled to every month, and then only sporadically.

While they waited, Rose described her job in glowing terms and highlighted the good parts of city life. AnaMary lifted her eyebrows at the contrast between the experiences she'd recounted to her sister earlier. But her half smile let Rose know she understood.

By the time Rose finished, Mamm's hand was trembling on hers. Rose leaned closer to her. "Have you had anything to eat recently?"

"I don't know. I was fixing lunch when . . ."

Rose got up from her chair. "I'll be right back." She asked for directions to the nearest vending machines. She didn't want to wait in long lines in the cafeteria in case she missed news about Daed. She brought back several snacks and drinks and distributed them to Mamm and AnaMary.

A little color came into Mamm's cheeks as she ate and drank some water. "How long do you think it'll be before we hear anything?"

Rose wished she could give a definitive answer, but as a nurse, she could think of so many possible scenarios and outcomes. She wanted Mamm to concentrate on the positive. "They need to get him stabilized and do some testing. It could be a while, depending on what they have to do."

She kept waiting for an opportunity to talk to AnaMary privately, but they couldn't leave Mamm alone. Her sister deserved to hear that Daed had said he loved her. Rose would leave out the part where she'd assumed Daed had meant the message for her.

Someone called out Eli Ebersol's name, and Mamm sucked in a breath. Rose took her arm and guided her over to hear the news. AnaMary trailed behind as if hesitant to know Daed's condition.

A woman in green hospital scrubs and holding a clipboard glanced over the notes. After introducing herself, she said, "Eli is in stable condition at the moment, but he's being scheduled for a triple bypass. They'll be taking him to room 218. You can go there to wait for him."

When she walked away, Mamm turned to Rose. "Triple bypass? What does that mean?"

"They'll make some new pathways for the blood to travel around the heart." Rose didn't want to tell her it would involve taking blood vessels from elsewhere in the body. The less she knew, the less she'd worry. "Bypasses generally are quite successful. I'm sure Daed will be fine."

"We should head to the room now." AnaMary started toward the hallway but stopped and looked at Rose. "Oh."

"Don't worry. I'm not going with you." Rose tried to keep the hurt from her voice but wasn't sure she was successful.

Mamm drew Rose into a bone-crushing embrace. "I'm so sorry about your Daed and all." She waved a hand vaguely. "But never forget I love you."

Rose blinked to prevent tears from falling. Daed might never forgive her, but knowing she had her Mamm's love meant the world to her. "I love you too, Mamm, and I'll be praying for Daed."

AnaMary hugged her. "I wish you were home for good. I miss you."

"I miss you too." She took a deep breath and, with a tear-clogged throat, she told her sister about Daed's words in the ambulance.

"Thank you for letting me know." AnaMary rubbed her eyes. "He's never said that aloud." She met Rose's gaze. "I wish he'd told you that too."

So do I. But Rose kept that sorrow to herself.

Rose reached into her purse for a pen and scribbled her cell number on a piece of paper. "Here, you can call me anytime." Rose gestured toward the chairs where they'd been sitting. "I'll stay here until you've seen Daed and know when his surgery is scheduled. I know he won't want to see me, but I'd still like to be as close as I can."

AnaMary nodded. "I'm so sorry. I want you to be there with us."

"I'd like to be, but I don't want to cause another heart attack."

AnaMary sucked in a breath. "Don't blame yourself for that. It's not your fault."

Rose waited until her Mamm and AnaMary disappeared into the elevator before making her way back to a waiting room chair. Her sister's words echoed in her head. *Don't blame yourself.* But Rose did.

12

Jonathan pushed open the entrance door to the emergency room, and Hannah bounced inside. He pulled her to one side, knelt, and put his hands on her shoulders. "I know you're excited about seeing Rose, but the hospital has sick and hurting people, so we need to be quiet."

Hannah sobered. "I'll be good."

He smiled at her. "I know you will." Before he could stand, an ambulance screeched up to the door, it's siren wailing.

Hannah clapped her hands over her ears and burst into tears. Jonathan scooped her into his arms and whisked her off to one side with her back to the entrance as EMTs wheeled in a patient. Maybe this wasn't such a good idea. Rose might not even be here, and Hannah had been through so much today.

All the people milling about the emergency room, the chaos, and the approaching ambulances all made him want to escape. He was used to people staring at his Amish clothing, but having a crying child in his arms made him even more conspicuous. Everyone in the waiting room seemed to be staring in his direction, including the Amish woman half-hidden by a pillar. She craned her neck to look past it.

Rose. He almost called out her name but stopped himself in time.

She beamed, got up from her seat, and hurried toward them. "Jonathan, what are you doing here?"

"Hannah was worried about you so I promised we'd come to the hospital to be sure you were all right."

"I'm more worried about her. Is she all right?" Rose reached out and rubbed Hannah's back.

Hannah lifted her head and peered behind her. "Rose?" She held out her arms, and Rose enfolded her in a hug.

Rose's kindness to his daughter overwhelmed Jonathan. He fought his attraction to her, yet every time he was around her, he found something new to admire. Jonathan kept his grip on Hannah, although she stretched between them. "She's too heavy for you."

"Don't be silly. I've lifted many patients, many much older and heavier than Hannah."

Because Rose was so petite and slender, Jonathan was reluctant to let her bear his daughter's full weight. "Are you sure?"

"I'm positive," Rose said.

When he let go, Hannah clung to Rose, wrapping her arms and legs around her. She laid her head on Rose's shoulder and sighed. "You didn't die."

"What?" Rose glanced at him with shocked eyes.

Jonathan winced. "Her Mamm left in an ambulance and didn't return. When you climbed into the ambulance and it drove off, she assumed . . ."

"Oh no. I'm so sorry I scared her that way." She stroked Hannah's back. "I'm fine, sweetheart. Nothing to worry about. It seems I've upset a lot of people today. First Martha, then Daed, now Hannah. Oh, and you. Did I make you late for your deliveries?"

"Everything got delivered in time, so please don't worry about that. As for the others, all of those were out of your control, so don't blame yourself for any of them."

"In spite of what you and AnaMary said, I do blame myself for Daed. If I hadn't come around the corner when I did, he wouldn't have gotten so angry."

"I was the one who started it. What was I thinking, trying to wrestle the lawn mower away?"

"You were thinking he shouldn't be out there mowing the lawn, and you were absolutely right."

Jonathan motioned to the seat she'd left. Several chairs had emptied on either side of it. Rose nodded and headed back to where she'd been. Her cheeks red, she picked up the cell phone on the chair beside where she'd been sitting. She clicked it on, checked it, and unplugged it. Then she sat in the chair with Hannah in her lap.

"Is it charged now?" Jonathan asked as she dropped the phone and charger into her purse. When she looked startled, he laughed. "You'd be surprised to know some men in our *g'may* have cell phones now. Most hide them, but it's becoming more common. The bishop's against them, but he hasn't banned them yet because some employers require them."

"Really? How do they charge them with no electricity, or has that changed since I left?"

"No, we haven't hooked up to electricity. Some people have solar, and others use their buggy batteries for power."

Rose appeared dumbfounded and shook her head. "I'd think cell phones would be considered more worldly."

"They probably are, but the community was unprepared for appliances that weren't hooked up to wires. They had no ordinances against them, but not all of us believe it's wise to use the world's technology."

"I should think not." Rose giggled. "I guess that's hypocritical of me, isn't it? I use a cell phone but don't think others should." Her expression grew serious. "I'm a cucumber in a potato patch—a problem wherever I go. I'm too Amish for New York. Even when I try to dress and act like everyone else, I don't fit in. They say I'm much too conservative."

"I'd think that's a good thing." Jonathan wasn't quite sure why, but he was relieved to know she hadn't become worldly.

"Then I come here, and I realize I'm not conservative enough. I dress Amish, but I find myself questioning things. Then I feel more Englisch than Amish. I feel like I don't belong anywhere."

Jonathan bit his tongue before he said she belonged with him. He needed to distance himself from her. Whenever he was around her, she drew him in until he forgot about her being Englisch, and that was dangerous.

Rose regretted telling Jonathan her inner feelings. Holding Hannah and being with him made her feel at home in a way she never did in New York or even here at home. Jonathan had always been easy to talk to, to confide in. Until he'd started courting Esther. Everyone thought Rose and David would be a couple, but Rose enjoyed her friendship with David because it meant she could spend time with Jonathan. He never acted like she was a pest when she tagged after him. For a time, she'd thought Jonathan might ask to court her when she joined the church, but then, before she started baptismal classes, he started dating Esther. Heartbroken, she'd fled.

Jonathan's voice came to her from far away. "Rose, are you all right?"

"What?" She dragged herself from the past back into the hospital waiting room.

He leaned closer, bringing her fully into the present, where she was hyper-focused on him—the rise and fall of his chest; the deep breaths in; and the soft breaths out, so unlike her own ragged breathing.

She shifted Hannah in her arms, surprised by how quiet she'd been.

Jonathan glanced at his daughter with love in his eyes. "She fell asleep soon after you took her. I'm sure Martha will be pleased she took a nap. Two, actually. She slept in the wagon too."

Rose was pretty sure Martha wouldn't be pleased if she knew where Hannah was napping right now. Rose had been so lost in her conversation with Jonathan and in her reverie, she'd missed all the signs of Hannah's sleep—the heaviness of her body, the slow breathing, and the lolling of her head.

"Do you want me to take her?" Jonathan asked. "She gets heavy when she sleeps."

"I'm fine, but thanks."

"Rose?" AnaMary rushed over to her. She stopped and stared at Jonathan.

"Hello," he said. "I came to see if all of you needed a ride home."

"How kind. That's what I came to talk to Rose about." AnaMary turned to Rose. "Daed's surgery is scheduled for eight tomorrow morning. Mamm doesn't want to leave tonight, so she's going to sleep in the chair by his bed. I'd stay too, but the chickens need to be fed and . . ."

Rose held up a hand. "You stay with Mamm. I'll take care of your chores tonight and tomorrow."

"But you were catching the train today."

"Family is more important, and I have vacation time." Rose wanted to help in whatever ways she could. After hearing AnaMary's frustrations in the garden, Rose wished Daed would let her help. Now she had her chance.

"Oh, Rose." AnaMary leaned forward as if she were going to hug her, but stopped. "I don't want to wake Hannah."

"I'll take her." Jonathan lifted Hannah from Rose's arms. "I'm amazed that she can sleep through all this noise and confusion."

Rose stood and hugged AnaMary. She still struggled to believe her eleven-year-old sister was now old enough to marry. Though she'd grown up, she still had the same loving heart.

When Rose stepped back, her sister's eyes were teary. "Thank you. Even having part of a day away from chores is *wunderbar*." She turned to go. "I'd better get back to Mamm, but I forgot to tell you. The staff said you saved Daed's life. If it hadn't been for your quick intervention, he would have died."

Rose collapsed in the chair. She'd only done her job, but she shuddered to think what might have happened if she hadn't been there.

Jonathan turned to her, admiration shining in his eyes. "I meant to tell you earlier how impressed I was by how competent you are. You knew exactly what to do and did it, and you must have been exhausted, but you kept going until the ambulance arrived. The hospital where you work is lucky to have you."

"Danke," she said shyly. "I only did what I was trained to do." Even if it was Hochmut, Rose had always longed to hear her Daed say she'd done something right, but he never had. Jonathan's approval meant the world to her.

When Rose's cheeks flushed that becoming shade of pink, she looked so sweet. All Jonathan wanted to do was take her in his arms and hold her tight. He was grateful Hannah was here to deflect that impulse.

Being around Rose, he lost all sense of time, but he knew it must be getting close to milking, so he stood and readjusted Hannah to a more comfortable position. "Are you ready to go? I'd be happy to take you home."

A smile blossomed on Rose's face. "I'd appreciate it."

Whenever he was around her, she brightened his day. She'd done that when she was younger, and even after living in the Englisch world, she hadn't lost her gift. As much as he would have liked to stay there basking in her sunshine, he had work to do.

They walked in companionable silence to the wagon. After Rose climbed in, Jonathan handed Hannah to her so he could untie the horse and drive. When he clucked to the horse, the wagon started with a jerk. Hannah's eyes popped open, and she smiled at her Daed and Rose. She wriggled off Rose's lap and squeezed between the two of them. Her nonstop prattling kept them occupied the whole way to Rose's house.

When Jonathan let her out, he thanked her for being so kind to Hannah.

Rose laughed. "I enjoy her company. Thank you for the ride and to Hannah for the great conversation."

"I'll wait to be sure you get in," Jonathan said.

After Rose opened the front door, he called out, "*Ach*, wait," and hopped out of the wagon. He'd tied a tarp to protect the vegetables, and when he removed it, Rose's suitcase was still in the back. Telling Hannah to stay in the wagon, he tied up the horse, pulled the suitcase to the steps, then carried it up to the porch. This time when her hand touched his as she took the suitcase from him, he didn't flinch and back away.

"Are you nervous about staying here alone?" he asked. "I can pick you up after milking and take you to Martha's for the night."

"I'll be fine. I'm used to being on my own." She lived by herself in a tiny New York apartment. Besides, the last thing she wanted to do was impose on Martha again.

"If you're sure?" Jonathan appeared reluctant to leave.

"I'm positive." If it hadn't been improper, she would have invited him in for a while. Her New York friends would snicker if she told them that; they had men friends over anytime they wanted. But Rose didn't want to cause any gossip or harm Jonathan's reputation.

After he turned to go, she pulled her suitcase over the threshold and turned to wave to Hannah and Jonathan. When the wagon was out of sight, Rose shut the front door, turned, and took a deep breath.

The last time she entered, she'd been concentrating on Mamm and AnaMary, and then she'd been dragged into Daed's room, so she'd had no time to look around. Everything looked the way it had when she'd left seven years ago. Even her bedroom remained exactly the same, including the wooden furniture Daadi had carved and the nine-patch quilt Mamm had sewn. Rose walked around touching things and reminiscing.

She intended to tackle the chores, but first she wanted to do one thing. If she remembered correctly, whoopie pies were Jonathan's favorite dessert. Mamm should have all the ingredients on hand. Rose checked and found everything she needed. She baked the chocolate dough for the outer part of the cookie while she whipped the creamy white filling. Then she gathered the eggs and picked the ripe tomatoes. By the time she returned to the kitchen, the whoopie pies had cooled enough, so she spread filling on one side and sandwiched it with another.

Rose wrapped and packed them into a basket and set off for Jonathan's. Now that she didn't have to lug her suitcase, she could take the shortcut through the fields and woods. If he'd left for Martha's, she'd leave the basket at his door. But when she arrived, Hannah was standing by the barn door, and she launched herself at Rose.

She set down her basket and held out her arms. Rose picked her up and swung her around in a circle until Hannah was giggling so much she could barely breathe. Hannah's laughter was irresistible, and Rose joined her. When she glanced up, Jonathan had come to the doorway, where he stared at them with a strange look on his face.

13

Jonathan looked around for Hannah and couldn't find her, so he stepped outside. Laughter near the barn drew Jonathan's attention, and he couldn't take his eyes off Rose whirling around in a circle with Hannah in her arms. When they stopped, all out of breath and panting, their giggles increased.

Hannah usually stayed upbeat and happy, but Rose took his daughter's joy to new levels. He rejoiced for his daughter, who had been lonely for a mother figure but hadn't taken to Martha. Although he was grateful for Rose's tenderness and spontaneity, both of which Hannah craved, he didn't want his daughter to get too attached to a woman who soon would be leaving them. He worried another loss might be too much for Hannah to bear.

Rose's laughter died when their gazes met. Had his thoughts shown on his face? Or had she sensed his disapproval? He didn't want to hurt her feelings, but maybe if he explained his concerns, she'd understand. He'd have to wait for a time when Hannah wasn't around.

Setting Hannah on the ground, Rose picked up a basket near her feet. She held out her hand, and Hannah slipped her hand into Rose's, a picture that started an ache—an emptiness and sense of loss—deep inside. He wanted Hannah to have a relationship like that, but how could she have someone like that in her life unless he married? The ache grew when he realized that even if he did remarry, it could never be to Rose.

She smiled at him, but his somber thoughts kept him from reciprocating, and her smile wavered. He hadn't meant to hurt her, but the idea of losing her made it too hard to curve his lips upward.

Her eyes downcast, she walked over and handed him the basket. "I wanted to thank you for driving me."

"You didn't have to do that, but danke." He lifted the lid and inhaled. The whoopie pies inside had a "freshly pulled from the oven" scent that tantalized his taste buds.

"Thank you. Whoopie pies are my favorites." This time his smile was genuine, and she relaxed.

"I know. Are you done with milking?" Rose asked. When he shook his head, she offered to help. "I used to help Daed, and I feel responsible for keeping you from getting your chores done."

Rose pitched in to help, and Jonathan couldn't help thinking how wonderful it would be if they did this together every night, but he warned himself that he needed to guard against getting used to her help. She'd be gone soon.

His resolution was difficult to keep when she encouraged Hannah to help with the chores and worked alongside his daughter to teach her. Rose was so patient and broke tasks down to those Hannah could successfully accomplish on her own.

When they'd finished the milking, they walked out of the barn together, swinging Hannah between them, like a real family. Jonathan longed for a connection like that. If only Rose were Amish.

Although the milking was difficult, Rose enjoyed working alongside Jonathan and Hannah. Sometimes her thoughts wandered to the past. Suppose Jonathan had courted her; would she have joined the church and stayed Amish? Rose suspected she would have endured anything to be with Jonathan, including her father's wrath.

Hannah squealed and took off after one of the barn kitties. Rose loved Hannah's exuberance. "She's so lively." Rose quickly amended her comment when Jonathan looked hurt. "I meant that in a good way. She has lots of energy that she uses in positive ways." Rose kept walking. "I should get back home and finish some of AnaMary's chores before it gets too dark."

"Thank you for your help in the barn, and for these." He held up the basket of whoopie pies. "Hannah enjoyed your company too."

"Speaking of Hannah, Martha seems a little overwhelmed by childcare and lack of sleep." Rose tried to judge Jonathan's reaction before she said anything more.

"Do you think so?" He stroked his beard. "She claims she's not, but I've wondered. I don't know what else to do, though. She loves the children as if they were her own."

Rose had noticed that and wondered at Jonathan letting Martha usurp his power. He seemed to give in to her, even when his own instincts likely were correct. "She does love them, but does it bother you that she makes most of the decisions?"

"Sometimes, but she has them all day long, so I feel she should have a say in their care. I still haven't given her my final decision about keeping the children full time. I'm struggling with that. I miss them when they aren't here, but I want to do what's best for them. I especially miss Hannah's company, because she loves to do chores with me. She's good with the milking, but I can't keep her here during the day because she's too young to help tend the plants."

"I was wondering. . ." Rose got up her courage to propose a plan she'd thought of earlier as she'd walked over to his house. "Would you consider letting me watch the children while Daed's in the hospital?

With his condition, I suspect he'll be there at least a week. I could watch them here or at our house. Mamm adores children and so does AnaMary."

"You're so good with Hannah, but I worry about the children getting attached to you when you'll be leaving soon."

"I understand, but I'd love to take care of Hannah tomorrow while you're working."

Hannah bounded over in time to hear Rose's last comment. She jumped up and down and clapped. Then she wrapped her arms around Rose's legs.

"Careful, Hannah, let's not knock Rose over." Jonathan gently detached his daughter's arms from around Hannah's legs. "I don't know."

"Please, Daed?" Hannah tugged at Jonathan's arm. "I want to play with Rose."

He shook his head. "Martha says you need to learn to do chores."

"I'd be happy to do that as well. She can help with gardening and canning." The more she thought about having Hannah's company, the more excited Rose became. She had so much fun when she was around Hannah, and it would keep her from being lonely. She'd also had fun working with Jonathan. "I could help with the milking tomorrow morning and then take Hannah back with me."

"You'll get up at four in the morning and do milking to have Hannah's company?" When Rose nodded her head, Jonathan laughed. "How can I pass up that offer?"

Rose wasn't sure why she'd pushed so hard for a chance to take care of Hannah, but Martha's negativity reminded her of Daed, and Rose had once been as lively as Hannah. Many parents believed in encouraging their children's creativity, and Rose's training in the Englisch world had reinforced that concept.

What would her life have been like if Daed had let her express her exuberance instead of repressing it? Maybe she wouldn't have rebelled.

After Rose left, Jonathan berated himself for agreeing to her plan. Spending more time around her had been too tempting to resist. But he couldn't afford to let himself and his emotions get entangled with Rose when she would soon be leaving. He also didn't look forward to informing Martha that Hannah would be spending the day with him.

Although he'd started the milking later than usual, with Rose's help, he'd finished in time for dinner at Martha's. The aroma of frying grease wafted through the living room.

She looked pleasantly surprised to see him. "Two nights in a row? Are you sure you're doing all your chores before you come?"

"I'm sure." He wasn't about to tell her Rose had assisted. To his surprise, Hannah didn't mention Rose's name either. Had she sensed the animosity Martha had for Rose? Or was she overtired from her busy day?

The fried chicken and fried potatoes were delicious and warming. Jonathan had trouble keeping his eyes open. Hannah began yawning when she was only halfway through her dinner.

Martha pounced on that right away. "See what happens when she doesn't have a nap? She's going to fall asleep here at the table."

Jonathan debated about contradicting her, but if he didn't, she'd raise a fuss when he mentioned tomorrow's plans. "Actually, she had a nice long nap today. I suspect she's tired because she worked so hard when we did the milking."

Martha's sideways glance indicated she didn't believe him.

To change the subject, he asked about Libby and Amos. Soon Martha was recounting their days, and Hannah's tiredness was forgotten.

Jonathan waited until dinner was over to tell her he'd be taking Hannah home with him.

She was carrying plates to the sink. She slammed them onto the counter and whirled around. "I thought we agreed the other night that all three children would stay here at night."

Taking a deep breath, Jonathan adopted a firm tone. "We agreed I'd think about it. I said I'd give you my decision the next day, but with Rose here, that got delayed. I've decided I need to try different options to see what works best for me, for the children, and for you."

Martha looked as if she were about to burst into tears. "But we already know what works best. The children need consistency, a stable home life. They'll have that here."

"I agree, but I'd like to explore some other options."

"You don't trust us?" Martha snatched the dirty silverware from the stack of plates on the counter and clattered it into the sink.

"Of course I do." Jonathan drummed his fingertips on the table. Why did his sister-in-law contradict every decision he made? He should have asserted himself long before this.

David came to his rescue. "Jonathan needs to decide what's right for his children, Martha."

With a loud huff, she finished clearing off the table. "Am I allowed to heat Amos's bottle?"

Jonathan pushed back the bench. "I'd appreciate it, but I'd like to feed him." He rounded the table. "Come on, Libby, let's get you ready for bed."

Martha turned around and looked at him with tear-filled eyes.

The tears were worse than the huff because they made Jonathan feel guilty for wanting to spend time with his children. He tried not to think about it as he enjoyed the nighttime routine, but Martha's eyes haunted him. Was he being unfair to her by insisting on this time together? He tried to rationalize it by telling himself she had them for most of the day, but it didn't help.

When he came back from tucking Amos into his crib, Hannah

was curled up in a little ball on the sofa. Martha had covered her with a green-and-orange afghan. As he reached down to pick up his daughter, Martha came up behind him.

"No sense in taking her out in the carriage when she's that tired. I can carry her up to bed," she offered.

"Thanks, but we have plans for tomorrow," he said as he lifted Hannah into his arms.

"Daed," she whispered sleepily, "am I playing with Rose tomorrow?"

Martha's eyebrows shot up so high they created deep crevasses in her forehead. "Rose? I thought you took her to the station today."

All Jonathan wanted to do was run out the door. He didn't want to stay for an inquisition. "Her Daed had a heart attack, so she ended up staying here."

"And you're going to trust her with Hannah instead of me? After what she did?" Martha turned and headed to the bedroom. Right before she went through the door, she said, "Whatever you do, don't leave Rose alone with Hannah."

David stepped out on the porch with Jonathan as he walked out the door. "Martha is right about Rose being irresponsible. I hope you'll supervise them closely."

"I'm not sure that's necessary. She's a nurse now and very competent." Jonathan wished they could let the past go.

"One more thing," David said in a low voice. "I'm sorry Martha's been so clingy with the children lately. Please don't judge her too harshly." He shuffled his feet and stared at the ground, his cheeks crimson. "We don't usually talk about things like this, but she had another"—his voice dropped to a whisper—"miscarriage." He slipped back inside so quickly the screen door banged shut behind him.

David's explanation only added another weight to the heavy load of guilt Jonathan already carried.

14

When Rose returned home after being with Hannah and Jonathan, the emptiness of the house closed around her. Being at Martha's the past few days had reminded her of how lonely her life was in New York and in this house without her family. She missed sitting at a table full of people for every meal and talking, laughing, and sometimes arguing.

New York meant people rushing by or living in the same building, but they rarely connected. They all lived their separate lives. Even her nursing school friends hardly ever got together anymore. They all worked long hours, their schedules rarely matched, and some had moved to other parts of the country.

To banish her gloomy thoughts, Rose threw herself into the chores. She wanted to surprise AnaMary with a clean house, a weeded garden, and a mowed lawn. As Rose cleaned up the whoopie pie mess in the kitchen, her phone trilled. She hurried into the living room and dug through her purse. By the time she found it, the phone had stopped ringing.

She'd missed three calls from her supervisor. The messages, each one more frantic than the next, asked her to return early from her vacation. Several people were out with a terrible virus, so they needed her desperately.

Rose returned the call. Holding the phone against her shoulder, she listened to it ringing while she got out dinner ingredients.

"Hello," Sofia answered, out of breath and tense. "Oh, Rose, I'm so glad you finally called. We're so shorthanded here. Can you come back right away? You can take your choice of vacation dates to make up for it."

Rose was torn. She disliked letting her colleagues down, but who would do AnaMary's chores? "I'm so sorry, Sofia, but my father's having triple bypass surgery in the morning, and I need to be here to help my family. I don't know how long I'll be gone. I may need to take some personal time as well."

Rose busied herself with fixing dinner while her supervisor pleaded, cajoled, and finally threatened to replace her if she didn't return when she was scheduled. Rose tried to answer calmly, but she held firm until Sofia ended the conversation.

For the first time in a long time, Rose felt a sense of peace as she prayed for guidance. If God wanted her to return to her nursing job, He'd keep it open until she returned. Otherwise, she'd wait for His leading for her future.

Once she had the dinner casserole in the oven, she weeded until it grew too dark to see, and then she canned tomatoes until late at night. But making the casserole had given her an idea. She prepared baked oatmeal for the morning.

She fell into bed, exhausted but excited about the morning with Jonathan, and praying all would go well for her father's surgery.

When Rose arrived at the barn the next morning, Jonathan and Hannah were already working. She asked if she could put the casserole dish in the oven, and Jonathan told her to let herself in. She set the oven on low and joined them in the barn. After giving her a welcoming hug, Hannah instructed Rose all about how to milk cows. When Rose pretended to be learning all the information and waited for Hannah's advice before proceeding, Jonathan's eyes met hers over Hannah's head, and they shared a grin. As they had the day before, they worked like a team and soon were finished.

While Jonathan cleaned the equipment, Rose took Hannah inside and helped her set the table. When Jonathan came in, he sniffed the air.

"Ummm. I don't usually have time for breakfast. But with your help, I got done much earlier than usual."

"I-I should go." Rose had been planning to get everything ready and slip out before he came in for breakfast.

"Have a seat," Jonathan offered. "I doubt anyone saw you cutting through the woods, so your reputation should be safe."

"I'll just wait outside for Hannah." Rose hoped her words didn't sound as shaky as she felt. "If it's all right with you, I can take her with me to feed the chickens and horse, pick tomatoes, and do some canning while you take care of your vegetables."

"Martha worries about Hannah not learning to do chores, so that will be wonderful for her."

Hannah jiggled in her seat. "I want to go to Rose's house now."

"After you clean your plate," he reminded her. He motioned to the bench across from Hannah. "Are you sure you won't join us?"

"Thank you, but no. I have another baked oatmeal casserole waiting for me at home." She pushed open the door and walked onto the back porch.

In addition to her worries about both their reputations, Rose felt too nervous to sit across from Jonathan. What if she gave away her feelings for him?

Jonathan hadn't realized how much Rose had contributed to his happiness that morning until the door closed behind her. Without her, much of the glow left the room. If he had a helpmeet like Rose, he could manage both the dairy and the vegetables and still have time left over for his family. How wonderful it would be to have warm meals here every day, to hear his children laughing and playing outside while he worked knowing they were being well cared for, and to have them all under his roof at night. The only problem was that the person he wanted beside him at the table and in the barn was Rose.

Whenever he pictured her, she was in Amish clothes. His mind kept coming back to the same question: would he be as attracted to her if he saw her in Englisch clothing? Maybe that was a way to kill his yearning for her. He struggled to imagine her in the Englisch world, but all he conjured up was a puzzle with many pieces missing.

Rose's quiet voice drifted in through the window screen. She was on her cell phone. Her words sounded garbled, but she did say "Daed," so she must be checking on her father.

Jonathan didn't want to eavesdrop on a private conversation, so he turned to his daughter. "Stop dawdling, Hannah," he said gently. She seemed lost in a happy daydream, her fork poised in the air, talking to herself. "Rose is waiting."

At the mention of Rose's name, Hannah unfroze and dug into the remainder of her oatmeal. She gulped down the creamy milk Jonathan had brought in and jumped up from the table.

Before she raced out the door, Jonathan pointed to her cup and plate. "Be sure to put your dishes in the sink. I'll wash up today, but soon you'll be old enough to help."

Jonathan caught the screen door before it slammed shut and leaned to ask Rose how her Daed was.

"He was heading to surgery, so AnaMary promised to call when he's in recovery." Her face was wistful. "I wish I could see him afterward, but I don't want to cause another incident."

"I'm so sorry." Jonathan wished he could reach out and comfort her, but he kept one hand on the door and the other clamped to his side and fixed his eyes on his daughter. "I'll be praying for him while I work."

Rose smiled. "Danke." She took Hannah's hand, and the two of them walked toward the shortcut through the woods.

Jonathan stared after them until trees blocked them from view. He missed Hannah's cheery patter and Rose's calming presence as he cleaned up the kitchen, but he had a lot of work to do in the greenhouses today. Gardening left him plenty of time to daydream about Rose and Hannah working together.

By the time Rose returned that afternoon with Hannah, Jonathan had all his crates loaded in the wagon, ready for the next day's deliveries, and he'd pulled out the buggy to take Hannah to Martha's for dinner.

He walked partway along the path to meet them. "How is your Daed?"

The small worry lines he'd noticed beside Rose's eyes this morning had smoothed out. "The surgery was successful, and he's out of recovery. AnaMary couldn't talk long. She was on the public phones and wanted to get to his room. She'll call later tonight with an update. But they're expecting him to stay five days."

"I'm glad it went well. I hope you'll have more good news tonight."

"Thank you." Her low, sweet voice sent quivers through him, and he forced his attention away from her animated face.

Beside Rose, Hannah appeared about to explode. He must remember to thank Martha for teaching his daughter politeness. Although Hannah's wriggling made it clear she could hardly wait for her turn to speak, she didn't interrupt them.

"What did you do today?" he asked Hannah.

A torrent of words poured out so fast Jonathan could barely understand them, but two words stood out with great frequency—*help Rose.*

"It sounds like a busy day, Hannah. I hope you were a big help."

Rose placed a hand on his daughter's shoulder. "She certainly was."

"I'm glad, and I hope she wasn't any trouble." After Rose assured him she wasn't, Jonathan motioned to the buggy in the driveway. "Come, Hannah. We need to get ready to go to Martha's."

When Hannah tugged on Rose's hand to pull her in that direction, Rose shook her head and disengaged her hand. "Only you and your Daed are going."

The little girl's lips pursed in a pout. "I want you."

"Not tonight." Rose smiled. "You'll have fun with Libby and Amos."

"You're welcome to come along," Jonathan said. "Martha always makes extra, so she has enough for guests."

"Thank you, but I have dinner in the oven."

Hannah planted her feet and refused to budge. Jonathan bent and lifted her into his arms. She struggled and kicked until he could barely hold her. "I want Rose. Not Martha."

"Hannah." Jonathan's sharp tone halted her fussing. "You may not say mean things about anyone, especially not your Aenti." Then he softened his words. "I know you had a good time with Rose and want to spend more time with her, but Rose has other things to do tonight."

Hannah studied Rose with suspicion.

"I do have things to do tonight," Rose said, "but I'll see you tomorrow." She glanced Jonathan's way with a question in her eyes, and he nodded. "Good," she said. "Hannah and I had so much fun today."

Rose started to walk away but then hesitated and turned toward him. "Maybe this isn't the best time to ask about this, but with Daed gone for several days, I wondered if you'd like to give Martha a break. I'd be happy to help out with all three children."

"That's way too much."

Rose laughed. "When I worked in pediatrics, I had many children to care for, and some of them were quite ill. I can certainly help out with your three."

Jonathan stood for a minute staring off into space. "Martha won't like it, but maybe a break would be good for her, especially right now." He shifted Hannah to one side and stroked his beard. "Tomorrow might work well because I have deliveries. I could take Libby and Hannah with me all afternoon if you could handle Amos?"

Rose's delighted laughter made him certain she really did want to do this.

Jonathan continued, "The children can stay with me the rest of the day. I won't be doing gardening."

"I don't mind teaching the girls some chores." Rose smiled at Hannah. "I'll see you tomorrow at four in the morning for more milking lessons."

Hannah beamed. "I'll show you how to do it right."

Jonathan loved the way she interacted with his daughter, but he didn't want her to feel obligated to do the morning milking. "Rose, you don't have to do all this," he said.

Rose waved and headed toward the woods. "I'm looking forward to it."

Once Rose was out of sight, Jonathan placed Hannah in the back seat of the buggy and got in the driver's side. He dreaded telling Martha his plans. Maybe it would be best to plan for one day at a time rather than all at once. That way if tomorrow didn't go well, he could return the children to their regular schedule at Martha's. But he didn't want to give up without trying.

Jonathan waited until the meal was over and Martha was ready to take the children up to bed. "You know how we talked about possibly leaving the children here full time?"

"Yes." Martha's smile stretched wide on one side of her face, but the scarred side's stiffness constricted the smile on that side, making it crooked. Few things drew a full-fledged smile from Martha, and Jonathan hated to disappoint her. He should have found a better way to introduce his plan.

"I've been finding I miss the children at night. Hannah did quite well both last night and today, so I'd like to experiment with having all three of them tonight and tomorrow to see if it works."

"No!"

Martha's scream startled Libby, who was drifting off on the sofa next to Jonathan, and she started bawling. Hannah joined in, crying that she wanted to play with Rose. All he needed was for Amos to wake and join them. A few minutes later, his son obliged him.

Soothing all three of them took a while, and Jonathan wondered if Rose knew what she was getting herself into. Maybe this hadn't been such a good idea after all.

Rose hummed as she worked around the house that evening and waited for AnaMary's call. Having Hannah here today had been fun and eased Rose's loneliness, but every chore had taken twice as long as usual. After she'd demonstrated a chore, she tried to let Hannah do as much of the chore alone as she could, which took a great deal of patience and waiting. Most of the time, Rose had to finish, or redo the work when Hannah wasn't looking. But working with Hannah had been such a joy, she hadn't minded.

The phone rang, and Rose hurried to answer it. She loved hearing AnaMary's voice on the other end.

"Daed's doing very well. They even had him sit in a chair for a short while." AnaMary's voice changed to exasperated. "He's so impatient to get out of the hospital, though, and keeps bothering the nurses, asking when he can leave."

"Have they said how long he'll be there?"

"Anywhere from three to five days." She laughed. "He's tells them he needs to leave tomorrow so he can mow the lawn."

"I don't believe it." Rose shook her head but didn't join in AnaMary's laughter. The lawn. She'd forgotten all about that. The mower was still in the yard where Jonathan and Daed tussled. Rose made a mental note to add it to her chore list as soon as she got off the phone.

"Rose? Are you still there?"

"Sorry. I was thinking I'd better make sure the grass is cut before Daed's discharged."

"Smart idea. Then we won't have to worry about him trying to mow the lawn for at least another week. Although who knows what other jobs he'll feel are urgent. Maybe reroofing the chicken house or—" AnaMary stopped and said a muffled, "I'm sorry. I'm almost done." Then her voice rang clear as she rushed out her words. "Someone needs to use the phone, so I'll talk to you tomorrow, Rose." A loud click was followed by a buzzing sound.

Rose went to the kitchen and added lawn mowing to the chore list she'd jotted yesterday when she arrived. How she'd find time for that with helping Jonathan and taking care of AnaMary's chores, she had no idea. Right now she needed to sleep because milking time would be here soon, and she'd need all her energy to care for three little ones tomorrow.

Despite being exhausted after the day's work, Rose lay awake long into the night recalling Jonathan's words, smiles, and accidental touches. Her memories drifted into dreams that left Rose's pillow damp the next morning when she realized they weren't real. She shook herself from the fantasies at three and padded out to the kitchen to make breakfast for five. Then she packed sandwich ingredients for lunch and a casserole for dinner.

Her cell phone battery was low, so she took the buggy battery from the barn to charge it. Daed would be horrified to know what she was doing, but Rose knew she shouldn't be without a phone in case of emergency while she was watching the children. She also didn't want to miss AnaMary's calls.

Once the phone was charging and the meals were ready, Rose went to her room to dress. After years of Englisch clothing, which was so easy to slip on, arranging her dress and cape, tying on her black work apron, awkwardly twisting the sides of her hair back, and pulling her hair into a tight bob at the back of her head took longer than she'd anticipated. She hastily pinned on her Kapp, not sure if it was crooked. Then she grabbed the basket she'd packed and rushed toward Jonathan's, afraid she'd be late.

She needn't have worried. Jonathan stumbled out the door as she arrived, his eyes bloodshot and bleary. It looked as if he'd had a long night. Hannah and Libby each clutched one of his hands. Rose had been embarrassed by her own clumsy efforts to create her bob, but the girls had kerchiefs tied over messy hair, which had been pulled back into ponytails.

Catching her studying his daughters' hairstyles, Jonathan flushed. "I don't know how to do their hair as neatly as Martha does it. She tried to teach me, but the intricate motions are too much for my hands." He let go of the girls and held up his hands—large, strong, and tanned. Hands that Rose wished would close around her fingers or stroke her face.

She lowered her eyelids to hide her reaction, but her heated face likely gave it away. She thought her cheeks must have matched Jonathan's. "Would you like me"—her voice squeaked, and she swallowed, hoping to sound less nervous—"to do the girls' bobs?"

"That would be wunderbar. If you don't mind, that is." He sounded almost as tense as she was.

"I'd be happy to." She moved the basket handle higher on her arm so she could take their hands and tried not to think of holding his. "I, um, brought some food for meals."

The appreciation in his eyes started a tingling in her chest that spread through her body.

"Rose?" Hannah tugged on her hand several times before Rose managed to tear her gaze away.

"Y-yes?" Rose knelt in front of Hannah to focus her attention.

"Are you going to fix our hair?" At Rose's nod, Hannah blew out a breath. "That's good. Martha says messy hair and rooms are signs of disrespect toward God."

Did a four-year-old even know what *disrespect* meant? Or was she just parroting Martha's words? Rose didn't want to contradict Martha, but she wanted to ease Hannah's worries. "I think God understands if Daeds don't know how to fix hair."

"Oh, good." Hannah's tight face relaxed.

Jonathan chuckled and mouthed a thank-you as Rose stood and led the girls inside.

Rose wasn't sure how much better she'd be at fixing the bobs, but she determined to try. Did God understand if ex-Amish girls didn't do a good job either? Rose suspected God might, but she was certain Martha wouldn't.

She tucked the food into the almost-empty refrigerator and set to work on the girls' hair. By the time she'd finished, the girls' bobs were only slightly sloppier than her own. She'd wanted to do her best, but she'd failed. Perhaps suggesting Jonathan bring the children home had been a bad idea. His exhaustion this morning likely meant he hadn't gotten enough sleep. That was all her fault.

Rose was about to lead the girls out to the barn when Amos squalled. She opened the back door and sent Hannah and Libby out to the barn. "Hannah, take your sister's hand, and be sure she stays safe."

Hannah's chest swelled with pride. "I can do that. I know all about barn safety."

"I know you do," Rose said. "You taught me a lot yesterday." Martha would probably chastise Rose for encouraging Hannah's Hochmut, but in this, Rose's heart leaned toward Englisch ways. "Tell your Daed I'll feed Amos and bring him out."

As soon as the girls had descended the porch steps, Rose put a bottle on to heat and hurried upstairs. She passed several rooms with neatly made beds that Martha would surely approve before she came to the small room at the end of the hall.

Amos had pulled himself to his feet and clung to the crib rail as he bawled. Rose didn't want to startle him, so she said in a soft voice, "Hi, Amos, how are you? Would you like some milk?"

He stopped crying and stared at her with damp eyes. She lifted him from the crib and was pleased when he snuggled against her. After she'd changed and dressed him, she carried him downstairs for his bottle. She cuddled him close as he sucked on the bottle greedily. Then she headed out to the barn.

15

When Rose walked into the barn carrying Amos, Jonathan's heart stutter-stopped. She looked so beautiful standing there and, at the look of love on her face as she gazed down at Amos, he fought to draw in a breath.

He'd wanted his children home with him, but he'd made a mistake by including Rose. He could barely keep his attraction under control when he was around her, but seeing her with his children pushed him over the edge. How could he possibly interact with her normally? Put together coherent sentences? Keep his mind on his work?

And when she smiled, heaven help him, he wanted to take her into his arms and never let go.

"Jonathan?" Rose's breathy voice added to his temptation.

He stood so she could see him, and her lips curved up. Setting a hand on the cow's rump, Jonathan breathed in the animal odor, the hay, and the earthy barn smells. Anything to wrench his thoughts from Rose.

"Thank you for taking care of Amos." He managed to push out his words by keeping most of his mind on the cows and the chores.

"I was happy to. He's such a cutie." Rose started toward him, but Jonathan wasn't sure he could handle her closeness. Not right now.

He pointed to the far side of the barn, and she turned to look at the playpen he'd built when Hannah was a baby, so he and Esther could work together in the barn.

Esther. Jonathan repeated her name like a litany. He was still in his mourning period. He needed to remember that. And Rose was Englisch.

If only those concerns could override the pull he felt toward her. Why had God brought Rose back into his life when he was overwhelmed with loneliness? When he was too weak to withstand temptation?

"What a great idea!" Rose examined the gated area surrounded by wooden posts. Libby sat inside on a quilt, threading colored discs onto a wooden dowel. "Did you make this?"

"Yes." Jonathan's clipped answer sounded brusque.

Had she offended him? Perhaps she shouldn't have praised his handiwork. Amos sucked the last sips from the bottle. She held him upright over her shoulder and patted his back. While she waited for his bubble, Rose couldn't resist a peek at Jonathan.

She was surprised to catch him staring at her and sucked in a breath. If she wasn't mistaken, he was staring at her with the same yearning she had for him. His eyes flickered shut, and when he opened them again, his eyes and face were blank. Had she imagined that look? Most likely, her own attraction to him had caused her to see something that wasn't there. Rose faced the playpen again to hide her confusion.

Jonathan had enough to distract him without her moony stares making him feel uncomfortable. She had to keep her feelings from showing on her face.

Libby smiled when Rose lowered Amos into the play area, and Rose responded. Although she had to keep her reactions in check around Jonathan, she could show her love for the children. Libby didn't say anything, but she pointed to a padded wooden box in the corner. Rose lifted the lid and found several toys. *What a clever idea to make a seat and toy box.* Jonathan was so creative. He was a lot of other things too, but she wouldn't let herself go there.

She handed Amos a rattle and went over to help Jonathan with the milking. His neutral expression when he looked up convinced her she'd been mistaken earlier. The attraction she'd seen in his eyes had been nothing more than her overactive imagination.

She masked her disappointment and added a cheerful note to her voice to make up for her discouragement. "Where should I start?"

Jonathan's directions were competent and unemotional. He didn't even smile. Unless he was too absorbed in his work to look at her, it almost seemed as if he didn't want her around. Maybe she'd been too pushy, insisting on helping him with chores and children when he'd prefer to do them on his own.

Well, she was here now, so she'd be as useful as possible and stay out of his way. The two of them worked in silence, but Hannah's chatter filled the uncomfortable quietness. Rose again played along with her, letting Hannah explain how to do the milking.

After an hour of tension-filled muteness between the two of them, Jonathan called out, "Rose?"

Her heart pitter-pattered, anticipating a conversation. "Yes?"

"I forgot to ask about your Daed."

Rose tried not to let her disappointment show. "He's doing well. AnaMary says he's eager to get out and get home."

"I don't blame him for that. I'd probably feel the same way. I'm sure, knowing your Daed, he doesn't like being cooped up."

"That's for sure." Rose recounted her conversation with AnaMary and added, "My sister says he can't wait to get home so he can do the lawn."

Jonathan raised his eyebrows. "The lawn? He doesn't remember that's what started his heart problems?"

"I guess not." Rose nibbled on her lower lip. Daed might not remember struggling with Jonathan, but he'd surely recall his anger at her. The anger that had caused him to collapse.

"Are you all right, Rose?" Jonathan asked as he walked past.

"Just thinking about my Daed and wishing things could be different." After the ride in the ambulance, Rose had thought the two of them had connected. At least, until he said her sister's name.

Jonathan stopped, and the sympathy on his face almost brought tears to her eyes. He took a few steps toward her and lifted his arms as if he might hug her, but then he lowered them to his sides. "I wish you didn't have to go through that."

Her distress over Daed didn't come close to Jonathan's loss. Despite what he'd said about broken relationships, dealing with a spouse's death had to be devastating. The sorrow in his eyes when he gazed off into the distance revealed the hurt he was enduring. Yet, he'd taken time to comfort her. She could barely choke out her thanks.

When she did, Jonathan gave a brisk nod and turned abruptly. He went back to being distant and businesslike. His eyes stayed shuttered as if he'd retreated far into himself. Perhaps it was his sorrow, or maybe he'd seen her neediness and longing, and wanted to distance himself from her.

Rose tried not to let it affect her, but as the morning went on with no conversation from Jonathan, her loneliness increased. Hugs from Hannah and Libby helped, but Rose missed the connection she'd experienced when she talked about her Daed.

Jonathan suggested she feed the girls breakfast while he cleaned the equipment and the barn. She missed seeing him in his place at the table, but she could relax and be herself. Hannah helped her drag the high chair to the table so Amos could eat with them.

Rose was wiping Amos's sticky face and hands when Jonathan entered the kitchen. He stopped partway through the door. A sickish look crossed his face. Hurt flickered through Rose until it occurred to her that the last time someone had wiped Amos's face in this kitchen, it would have been Esther. No wonder he'd reacted like that.

She wanted to offer him breakfast, but she worried that, too, might remind him of Esther.

"I'll, um, just wash up." He strode through the kitchen and returned a short while later, his bangs damp.

He must have washed his face too. The wet ends made him look younger and more vulnerable, and Rose's heart went out to him. She hadn't intended to stir up sad memories.

She didn't want to carry over the plate she'd fixed for him, but he'd been up working and she knew he must be hungry. When she set it in front of him, he glanced up from the plate with that blank look he'd had earlier. Maybe he used it to cover his sorrow.

"Thank you," he said, but his tone was lackluster.

"If it's all right with you, I thought I'd take the children to my house, so you can have a break. It doesn't look like you slept much last night."

"I didn't. Amos woke once, and Libby and Hannah decided to sleep in bed with me, so my ribs are battered from small feet kicking me all night long." Jonathan's rueful expression as he rubbed his side made Rose giggle.

"I'm sorry; it really isn't funny," she apologized.

Her laughter had set off the girls, and soon they were all chuckling. It released the tension between them, and Jonathan returned to his usual friendliness.

"I'm going to insist they sleep in their own beds at night, so I can get a little rest." He directed a mock frown at his daughters that stirred up deep belly laughs. "I mean it," he said. "From now on, you both stay in your own beds."

When he looked over at Rose, his eyes sparkled, and once again, she sensed a deeper connection between them.

"I don't want to burden you with the children," he said.

"It's not a burden at all. I love being with them."

Jonathan inspected her face as if to be sure she was telling the truth. His eyes filled with admiration, he said, "If you're positive."

"I am," she insisted.

Hannah cheered, and after a glance at her sister, Libby joined in. "We can go to Rose's house!"

Libby echoed, "Go Rose's house!" She joined her sister in another loud cheer.

Jonathan smiled at them, and his eyes softened. That softness transferred when he met Rose's eyes, and she almost melted.

"Visiting your house seems to be popular, so I guess I'd better not decline, or I might have a major rebellion." He forked a bite of breakfast into his mouth and chewed. "Delicious. I planned to leave for the restaurant deliveries right after lunch, so I'll come to pick up the girls. Unless you want to come too?"

His invitation and smile seemed genuine. Rose didn't want to appear jubilant, but she didn't want him to think she was unenthusiastic either. "I'd like that." She'd enjoyed the last time, because it gave her a chance to watch him without feeling guilty. This time, she'd also have the children for company.

"Great. I'll pick you all up around noon."

"I'll feed the children before you come, and I left sandwich fixings in the refrigerator."

"You didn't have to do that."

"I don't mind. I figured you'd have enough to do, taking care of the children, so I brought meals. The dinner casserole just needs to be warmed for half an hour."

"Dinner too?" Jonathan looked overwhelmed. "I don't know what to say."

"You don't have to say anything. Nurses like to take care of people."

Jonathan's smile faltered and his friendliness vanished. His guard had gone back up, and Rose had no idea why. They'd been getting along so well.

The word *nurses* stabbed Jonathan in the chest. He'd been feeling so close to Rose and enjoying her company, he'd forgotten she was an Englischer.

All day long, he'd been up and down, like ocean waves pulled into the shore, then dragged back out again. Whenever he let himself get too close, the undertow yanked him back out again. He had become the man who "wavereth," one the Bible described as "a wave of the sea driven with the wind and tossed." That described him perfectly.

He tried to regain his equilibrium as Rose collected Hannah and Libby. She reached into her basket on the counter near the refrigerator and pulled out a long piece of heavy cloth, wrapped part of it around her, then picked up Amos and tucked him into the front folds. Her hands flashed as she flipped and draped and tied.

Rose's deft movements fascinated Jonathan. "What are you doing?"

"Making a baby carrier. I needed my hands free to take care of the girls." Her words were friendly, but he detected a tinge of hurt underlying them.

He wished he hadn't drawn into his protective shell like a turtle startled by a predator. "Very clever, but wouldn't it be easier to take them in the buggy?"

Rose tipped her head down so her eyes weren't visible. "I don't know how to drive one. Daed never let me try. Not a buggy, not even a pony cart. He said he couldn't trust me on the road, so he drove me everywhere."

"I see." Jonathan had a hard time understanding a parent who didn't teach his children how to drive. Most children drove pony carts by the time they were in elementary school. He'd never really thought about it before, but Rose had walked most places when they were young.

Rose and the girls waved to him and headed off. Jonathan wished he were going with them. He hadn't expected to have free time this morning, but he could work in the greenhouses. As he cared for his plants and picked ripe vegetables, an idea nagged at him. Rose had spent so much time helping him, he wanted to do something for her. He had the perfect idea. He cleaned up the kitchen, packed himself a lunch, and hooked up the wagon. He hoped he could keep it a surprise until he had finished.

Rose brought an old cradle up from the basement for Amos, padded it well, and put him down for a nap. He went right to sleep, and the girls helped her garden. Libby mostly stabbed a trowel into the dirt and dug holes. Rose put her in a bare area so she wouldn't disturb the plants, and she seemed content. Hannah wanted to be a real gardener, but she sometimes uprooted plants as well as weeds. Rose taught her to look for one particular weed, and her gardening skills improved. They didn't stay outside long, because Libby grew bored quickly.

They worked in the kitchen for a while, and other than Libby spilling sugar and Hannah getting eggshells into the cake batter while cracking eggs, the baking went well. With the red velvet cake in the oven, they whipped the frosting. The girls soon tired of whisking, and Rose took over. As her wrists grew tired and achy, she missed having an electric beater, but it was satisfying to cream icing by hand.

The cake layers were cooling on the counter when Amos woke.

Rose heated his bottle and fed him while the girls snapped the ends off the green beans. Libby enjoyed that and, other than breaking off too much on some beans, she did a good job. Then Rose wrapped Amos in the carrier again so she could help them finish. She could hardly concentrate on the chores in her excitement. Jonathan would be picking them up soon.

She sat at the kitchen table and let her mind wander. She visualized Jonathan's face the times they'd seemed to connect. She was so deep in memory, she thought she saw him in the yard outside. She shook her head and looked again. It was Jonathan.

She ran to the back door. He was mowing the yard with her Daed's push mower. The mower they'd fought over the other day.

"Jonathan, what are you doing?" she called.

He turned with a grin. "Don't want your Daed to worry about the lawn."

Rose went back inside shaking her head. With all the work he had to do, he'd still taken time to help someone else. That was one of the many reasons she'd fallen in love with him many years ago, and it was one of the reasons she still loved him. That love had never died.

16

After Jonathan finished the lawn, they piled into the wagon. Rose held Amos, and the girls squeezed in between her and Jonathan. To passersby, they appeared to be a family, and Rose wished they were.

On the way into the city, the rocking of the wagon put Libby and Amos to sleep. Hannah was such a chatterbox, Rose couldn't carry on a conversation with Jonathan. At each stop, she admired Jonathan's strong back and muscles as he carried the crates into the restaurant. By the second stop, Hannah had drifted off to sleep too.

Jonathan kept the conversation light and acted distant. Rose longed for the flashes of friendship—or perhaps something more—they'd shared from time to time. Instead, their talk grew stilted and polite. Having him so close physically yet so far away emotionally tore Rose apart inside.

They reached the third stop, and Jonathan climbed out, picked up some crates, and tripped on uneven pavement. The crates tilted, and small orange balls bounced out of the top one. Jonathan juggled the crates until he had them balanced again. Rose jumped out of the wagon and rushed over to gather the fallen vegetables. She adjusted Amos over one shoulder so she'd have a free hand and picked up the first one.

It resembled a miniature pumpkin with green stripes. "What is this?" she asked Jonathan as she placed it in the open crate.

"Turkish orange eggplant. Danke, Rose."

Rose was amazed by the unusual shape and color of the eggplant as she gathered the rest. She hadn't peeked under the tarp or paid much attention to the vegetables in the crates as Jonathan carried them into the restaurants. After he came out, she quizzed him about the vegetables. He grew animated as he described his rainbow carrots, purple cauliflower and asparagus, and lemon cucumbers.

They reached the last stop, and Jonathan held out a hand to help her out of the wagon. "If you're interested, I'll show you what I have for this restaurant."

He didn't let go of her hand after she'd reached the ground, and Rose reveled in his touch. She missed the warmth of his hand when he let go to untie the tarp, fold it, and stow it in a wooden box built into the back of the wagon. The lid fit down to make a seat. He'd made a matching storage bench for the other side.

Before Jonathan stacked the crates, he showed her some of the vegetables he'd mentioned earlier. "I also have romanesco. It's a combination of broccoli and cauliflower." He pointed to a crate that seemed to be filled with small green Christmas trees wrapped in cauliflower leaves.

Rose inspected each crate. "Pink carrots? I've never seen those before."

"I have all different colors. Yellow, purple, some look almost black. If you're interested, I can take you through my greenhouses and gardens. These are only a few of my specialty vegetables."

"I'd like that." Rose was excited to have found a subject they could discuss without Jonathan putting up a wall to block her out.

He returned and pulled two quilts from the other storage seat and spread them on the wagon floor. He wrapped Hannah and Libby snugly in the quilts and closed the end gate. The whole way home, they discussed vegetables, and Jonathan explained the specialized techniques he used.

When they reached the country and the roads grew less crowded,

Jonathan pulled over to the side of the road. He got out, came around to Rose's side, and reached for Amos. A puzzled frown on her face, Rose handed him the baby. He wrapped Amos in a quilt and laid him in the small space above his sisters' heads.

He returned to Rose's side of the wagon. "Now scoot over."

Rose stared at him blankly. "That's the driver's side."

"Exactly." Jonathan couldn't resist a teasing smile. "That's where you sit when you learn to drive."

"You're serious?"

"It's time you learned. You never know when you might need to drive a buggy."

Rose giggled, imagining herself with a buggy in New York. "If I do this, you have to promise to take a subway with me."

"Sounds fun." His comical expression made her laugh harder.

She stopped laughing when he handed her the reins. He leaned close and wrapped his hands around hers to demonstrate the grip. With one arm around her shoulder, his chest against part of her back, and his arms rubbing against hers, Rose struggled to draw in a breath.

Jonathan helped her lift the reins and slap them lightly on the horse's back. With a jerk, the horse took off and Rose tumbled back, hitting Jonathan's solid chest. He tightened his arms around her, and Rose sighed. Even if she never learned to drive a buggy, she'd remember this lesson forever.

Jonathan pulled into his driveway after dropping off Rose, missing the warmth of her body in his arms. He'd enjoyed every mistake she'd made because it gave him the opportunity to hold her closer, to have her slide against him, to tighten his grip. With the reins in his hands, he still sensed the warmth of her hands under his. He wished he didn't have to wake the little ones. He'd like to sit quietly reliving the driving lesson.

Someone was sitting in a rocker on the front porch, and his heart leaped as he remembered discovering Rose on his porch the other night. Unfortunately, this time it wasn't Rose. It was Martha.

He waved and drove past her parked buggy to the barn, hoping to delay having to face her. Some of the joy he'd experienced after spending the afternoon with Rose leaked out.

With Amos in one arm, he had a hard time helping Libby and Hannah down from the wagon. Before he could open the back door for them, Martha swept Amos from his arms.

"I'll take care of the girls," she declared in a voice that brooked no argument.

Jonathan hesitated to turn the children over to her, but he had to take care of the horse and pull the wagon into the barn. After he was done, he headed into the house in time to hear Hannah exclaiming about how much fun she'd had at Rose's. His stomach sank.

Martha's glare left him in no doubt about her opinion. She'd question his judgment. He only hoped she wouldn't do it in front of the girls.

She stood and beckoned to his daughters. "I'll take Amos upstairs and put him in his crib. You girls come with me. I want you to play in your rooms so I can talk to your Daed."

Her emphasis on the word *Daed* left no doubt she would have preferred to substitute another word. Perhaps *imbecile* or *fool*.

While Martha was upstairs, Jonathan slipped Rose's layered hamburger casserole into the oven. At least he could impress Martha with the fact that he was feeding them properly. He only hoped she didn't question him about whether he'd made it himself. Although at this point, it didn't matter. She already knew the children had been with Rose.

Martha stomped downstairs and into the kitchen. "I can't believe you let the children spend time with Rose. You know she's irresponsible. I don't want them to get hurt. In the past eight months, I've come to love these children as if they're my own."

Yes, Jonathan had noticed that. In fact, it had gotten to the point where she wanted to determine everything they did. He didn't want to hurt Martha's feelings, but they weren't her children. Remembering her recent miscarriage, he couldn't challenge her, though. His children filled a void for her, and he didn't want to take them away.

Martha continued, "If anything happened to them, I'd . . . I don't know what I'd do. They mean the world to me. Please, please keep them away from Rose."

Jonathan couldn't make that promise. They had plans for tomorrow. He said the only thing he could. "I'll be very careful not to put them in dangerous situations."

Martha's long, slow exhale told him she was relieved. "I'm glad to know they won't be around Rose anymore."

He hadn't said that, and he knew he should correct her misunderstanding, but she cut him off before he could explain.

"I came to get the children for dinner. I'll take them now and see that they get to bed on time."

Jonathan didn't want to disappoint her, but he wanted this time with his children. "I have dinner for them in the oven. I've been trying to give you a break, let you get some rest."

Teary-eyed, Martha stared at the stove. "You have dinner for them? I made a meal. I don't want a rest. I want their company."

Jonathan hadn't meant to hurt her. He'd thought time away from the children would help. Once Rose left, he'd need Martha's help during the day. "It's only for a few days. I hoped you'd get some good sleep."

"A few days? You're sure?"

"Of course. I'll still need you to watch them during the day."

Martha glanced at him, and a smile spread across her face. "I can last a few days if I know Rose isn't going to be around them."

"But she . . ."

Sweeping on as if she hadn't heard him, Martha said with a wistful note in her voice, "May I take them home tonight?"

"I told you I'd like to try taking care of the children myself."

With a loud sigh, Martha pursed her lips together. "If you change your mind, let me know." She banged out the door.

Jonathan called the girls down for dinner. The meal seemed much lonelier without Rose. Even Hannah seemed subdued.

Later as he was tucking the girls into bed, Hannah asked, "Will Rose come tomorrow?" After Jonathan assured her Rose would be there, she grinned. Then her brow furrowed. "Aenti said we'll never see Rose again."

"Your Aenti was mistaken. Rose promised to come tomorrow." She was eager to see his vegetables while the girls napped.

Hannah's excitement mirrored his own. "I can't wait."

Neither can I.

Jonathan fell into bed that night torn between elation over seeing Rose tomorrow and guilt because his attraction to her grew stronger every minute he spent with her. He could tell he had hurt her with his brusqueness earlier in the day, but he'd tried to put up a barrier between them because he was fighting the desire to take her into his arms. He'd had that opportunity when he taught her to drive, and now it was all he could think about. He tried reminding himself Rose was Englisch and she was leaving soon, but pictures from the day flooded his mind and senses. He was playing with fire and would end up burned, but he couldn't manage to quench that spark.

Rose was washing her dinner plate and glass when someone knocked on the door. She'd told Jonathan she'd be happy to have the children overnight if he needed sleep. He'd insisted he'd be finc, but maybe he'd changed his mind.

She rushed to the front door and pulled it open. "Martha?" Rose hoped that didn't sound as unwelcoming as she felt. She pulled the door open wider. "Won't you come in?"

"What I have to say won't take long." Martha marched across the living room and settled on a hard-back chair. "First of all, I wondered how long you planned to stay. I understood Jonathan was taking you to the station the other day."

"I did plan to go then, but Daed had a heart attack."

"I'm sorry to hcar that." Martha looked as if she meant it. "Do you know how long you'll be staying?"

"Not yet. I'll leave when Daed is discharged. Most patients with bypasses at our hospital go home within three to eight days."

"So you'll go back to New York then?"

"I planned to. I need to get back to my job." If she still had her job.

Martha leaned forward and fixed Rose with a glare. "You're Englisch now, and you intend to leave soon. Do you think it's right to toy with Jonathan's affections when he's so lonely and vulnerable after losing his wife? And it isn't good for the children to get attached to someone who will soon be leaving. They've had enough grief after their Mamm's death." She added bitterly, "Not that you care what happens to others after you leave."

That wasn't true. Rose did care, but maybe Martha was referring to the past. Was some of Martha's anger because Rose left?

Martha narrowed her eyes. "I'm not only worried about the children emotionally. I worry about someone like you watching them."

"I have nurse's training, and I do my best to take good care of them."

Martha sniffed. "You can't be trusted to take care of anyone." She stood and started for the door.

Rose stood too and drew herself to her full height. Martha's words stung. "I don't understand why you're so sure I can't be trusted."

One hand on the doorknob, Martha turned. "Cowards run away when they can't face the truth of what they've done." She opened the door and stalked off.

The slamming door reverberated in Rose's ears the way Martha's criticism rang in her mind and heart. Rose mulled over what Martha said, and although she didn't understand Martha's final words, she did agree she shouldn't get close to the children if she was leaving. Hannah's fears when Rose went in the ambulance showed the depth of their bond. A bond that had only grown stronger. A bond Rose was about to break when she returned to New York.

To a child Hannah's age, Rose's leaving would be the same as a death. Hannah would never see Rose again, just like she'd never see her Mamm again. Martha was right. Rose needed to stay out of their lives.

As she prepared meals to take to Jonathan's, Rose's mind wandered to yesterday. Riding in the wagon together had increased her desire for a family and to be with Jonathan. She closed her eyes and felt his arms around her, and her pulse tripped faster. Had Jonathan felt the same sensations, or was he only being thoughtful in teaching her to drive? Even if he had experienced the same feelings, he'd only marry someone Amish. Could she give up nursing to return to the Amish?

Rose shook her head. She couldn't join the church for Jonathan, hoping he'd marry her, because that might never happen. And it wouldn't be a true profession of faith. If she bent her knee, it needed to be a decision between her and God.

17

Rose woke the next morning, uncertain whether or not to go to Jonathan's. She'd agreed to be there and didn't want to break her promise, but last night Martha had made her realize how much she was hurting the children and Jonathan. Not to show up today, though, would hurt Hannah and might remind the little girl of the suddenness of her Mamm's death. Children that age didn't know the difference between abandonment and death.

Maybe if she went over this morning, she could ease the transition by explaining her plans and preparing Hannah for her departure, although she didn't know exactly when that would be. First, she had to find out when Daed would be coming home.

As much as it pained her, she needed to make her break with Jonathan and his children today. The longer she let things continue, the more painful it would be for all of them when she left. Anxiety pooling in her stomach, Rose tucked the dinner casserole along with breakfast and lunch ingredients in a basket and left the house.

Hannah ran to greet her and threw her arms around Rose's legs as she usually did. But rather than bending down to embrace the little girl, Rose only smiled at her and headed for the kitchen with the basket. With every fiber of her being, Rose wanted to cuddle Hannah, but she made up her mind to step back and withdraw.

Hannah didn't seem to notice. She followed Rose to the kitchen, chattering the whole way. Rose did her best to paste a smile on her face as if she were listening, but she was busy searching for a way to tell Jonathan and Hannah. Trying to distance herself from this little girl she'd come to love ripped her apart inside.

Hannah bounced over to the counter. "Can I help?"

A lump in her throat, Rose nodded. She stopped herself from reaching out and setting a hand on Hannah's shoulder. Instead she stepped back and put the basket on the table so Hannah could reach inside.

"Everything in there goes in the refrigerator. Can you do that?"

Hannah nodded enthusiastically and began unloading the items in the basket. One by one, she put each one in the refrigerator. The only good thing about the painstakingly slow process was that it delayed seeing Jonathan. As Hannah proudly carried the ingredients to the refrigerator, Rose blinked away the moisture in her eyes. How would she ever say goodbye? To Hannah? To Libby and Amos? And most of all, to Jonathan?

Hannah finished her task and reached for Rose's hand. Rose pretended to adjust her apron and headed for the door, but when Hannah kept pace with her, her arm still outstretched, Rose couldn't resist taking the small warm hand in hers. How could something as simple as holding a child's hand turn your world upside down?

Jonathan had wrestled with his conscience most of the night and had woken more exhausted than if he'd been up all night with the children. In his heart, he knew what he had to do, but finding the courage to do it? He prayed that God would direct him to find the right time and the words to say.

He'd been unwise to get emotionally involved with Rose. The

Amish custom of a one-year mourning period was in place for a reason—to keep a widower from making foolish mistakes. When a man was lonely and grieving, it was much too easy to get involved with someone unsuitable. And to get his heart broken again.

Not to mention the damage to his children.

When Hannah rushed from the barn, Jonathan guessed Rose had arrived. They were gone for quite a while before they entered the barn, hand in hand. His pulse skyrocketed despite his decision to act otherwise. No amount of logic could cool his internal temperature whenever he was around her.

Rose lifted a hand in greeting but didn't meet his eyes. She went straight to work. He was grateful for her help, and she'd leave a gaping hole when she was gone, but it would be better for all of them. They finished the milking, and Rose went in the house to prepare breakfast as she had before while he cleaned equipment. They'd already developed a routine they'd need to break.

When he returned to the house, the aroma of bacon filled the air, but the kitchen was empty. Rather than feeling relieved, he felt bereft. He missed her presence filling the room with sunshine. Hannah was gone too.

He panicked until he heard her soft voice cooing to Amos. A sense of peace pervaded the house, as if everything was as it should be. *No, that wasn't right.* He had to stop indulging his fantasies.

By the time he'd washed up, Rose had returned to the kitchen. Amos was in his high chair, eating small bits of banana. Hannah and Libby sat at their places, hands in their laps, waiting for the prayer, while Rose bustled from the stove to the table, dishing out bacon, scrambled eggs, and hot-from-the-oven cinnamon rolls.

Once again, she refused to eat with them and went outside to sit on the porch. He had no idea why she worried about his reputation during breakfast, but she cooked and cared for Amos. Perhaps she wanted to avoid being around him.

That didn't make sense either. Until today, she'd been comfortable in the barn, and yesterday . . . She didn't protest during the driving lessons, and several times she seemed to be snuggling closer. Although that might have been his imagination.

After Jonathan rose from the breakfast table, Rose entered the kitchen. "We need to talk."

Jonathan nodded. "I can do the dishes later. Hannah, please take Libby upstairs and play in your room. I need to talk to Rose."

Hannah thrust out her lip. "I want to talk to Rose too."

"I know you do, and you'll have your turn later." Jonathan knew he shouldn't be speaking for Rose. He glanced over at her to be sure it would be all right. To his relief, she nodded. He didn't want to do this alone.

Rose cleaned Amos's hands and face and carried him upstairs to his room. When she came back down, she sat on a chair facing him. "You look tired. Were the children up a lot last night?"

"No." The only thing that kept him awake was his conscience. Realizing how abrupt his answer had been, he tried to soften it. "Actually, none of them woke up last night for the first time in months."

"That's good." Rose looked at him as if expecting him to say more, but when he didn't, she took a deep breath. "Martha stopped by last night to talk to me."

Jonathan's fists clenched. In addition to controlling his children, Martha seemed to want to control his life. He relaxed his hands. Any relationship he and Rose had was all in his mind. Martha's concern had been the children.

"Anyway," Rose continued, "Martha had a good point. She's afraid your children might get too attached to me, and my leaving will be like . . . like your wife's death."

Jonathan placed a hand across his forehead, shading his eyes. He pressed his fingers to his temples to relieve some of the pressure building up behind his eyes. Losing Esther had been an agony he never wanted to repeat. The children, especially Hannah, hadn't recovered yet.

"I'm sorry." Rose's tone was sympathetic. "I didn't mean to remind you."

Too choked up to respond, Jonathan waved a hand to let her know it wasn't her fault.

"I thought it might be best to explain to Hannah that I'm leaving, and then not see the children again after today."

"I agree." Jonathan forced the words out quickly before he could beg her to stay. Dealing with losing Rose would be hard for Hannah but equally as difficult for him.

Rose blinked at his rapid answer. Had he detected a bit of hurt flashing in her eyes? It disappeared before he could be sure. He hadn't meant to make her feel unwelcome.

She recovered and, looking him straight in the eye, asked, "Should we tell them now?"

Jonathan tapped his thumb against his lip as if deep in thought. "Why don't we wait until after the evening milking? That way I'll have more time to deal with Hannah's reactions. Libby will likely cry too, but she's easier to distract."

Rose opened her mouth to answer, but her cell phone rang. She fished around in her purse and lifted it out. "Hello . . . AnaMary." She stood and walked out to the back porch.

Jonathan filled the sink with hot water and plunged his hands in to wash the dishes. His intention hadn't been to eavesdrop, but Rose's voice floated through the window.

"That's great news."

The enthusiasm in her voice sounded forced, and Jonathan wondered what her sister had said. A short while later, she entered the kitchen.

"Daed's being discharged tomorrow afternoon, so I'll be leaving tomorrow morning."

"That's wunderbar about your Daed." Her leaving was good news because he'd avoid temptation. So why did it make him so sad? "I guess you'll be happy to get back to your job and New York."

"Yes," she said with hesitation. She didn't look any happier than he felt.

"What time do you want to leave? I can drive you to the station." Jonathan couldn't believe he'd blurted out that offer.

"No no, that's all right. I can call a taxi."

"Oh. I thought maybe Hannah and Libby might like to see you get on the train. Maybe it would help them understand you're going away, not . . ." Not dying. But she was going away forever.

Rose pressed her lips together and fought back tears. Saying goodbye to all of them at the station would be one of the hardest things she'd ever done. She'd probably bawl the whole way back to New York. If it would help the girls, though, she'd do it.

She tried to keep her voice steady. "In that case, I accept your kind offer." He'd also asked about time. She didn't know what his Saturdays were like. "Whatever time suits your schedule would be fine. Daed will be discharged around two, so I'd like to leave before he gets home."

"Would noontime work?"

"Perfect." Except it wasn't perfect, not at all. How could she leave all this behind? It wasn't like she could come back for a visit. She'd never see them again. Never.

Rose stood there, staring at the floor. Part of her wanted to run away and avoid facing Hannah and tomorrow's ride. Another side of her wanted to forget about nursing and New York and stay here forever.

"Rose?" Jonathan's voice penetrated her confusion.

She refused to meet his eyes. If she did, she'd give away her longings. "I'm sorry. I have a lot to think about and to get ready for tomorrow." In spite of the long list of chores she wanted to accomplish, she still wanted to spend time with the children. "May I take the children with me?"

"Of course, but wouldn't you get more done without them underfoot?"

That brought a smile to Rose's face. She definitely would, but having their company made the chores less onerous. "Probably, but I enjoy their company, and they're good helpers. Besides, you finished one of the hardest jobs on my chore list yesterday—mowing the lawn."

A short while later, with Amos wrapped in the makeshift carrier, and taking the girls by the hand, Rose was ready to set off.

"Wouldn't you like to drive the buggy?" Jonathan teased.

Rose turned away so he couldn't see the heat that suffused her face. "I don't think so."

"You were doing pretty well yesterday." His laughter followed her to the shortcut.

Why did he have to remind her of that? The whole way home Rose recalled the warmth of his body against hers, his hands over hers. She remembered nothing of the instructions about using the reins, only the touch of his arms and chest.

As she approached the house, she shook off the memories and concentrated on the chores she needed to do. First, they'd wash all the bedding so it could dry in the sunshine. Then they'd finish up the weeding so AnaMary could concentrate on taking care of Daed.

With Amos sleeping in the cradle, Rose took the sheets to the basement, filled the tub of the wringer washer with hot water and soap, and started the gas engine to spin the agitator. A loud rumbling filled the basement, and the sheets tumbled in the tub. Rose and the girls cleaned the house until the load was ready for the wringer. Rose kept a close eye on the girls.

First, she put the sheets through the wringer into a sink filled with hot rinse water. She let Hannah stand on a chair and push the clothing around with a plunger.

"Don't splash any, Hannah," she warned. "The water's hot enough to burn."

When the soap had been rinsed out, Rose ran the sheets through the wringer again, dropping them into the clothes basket. Libby stood on tiptoe and pointed as the clothes came out the other side of the wringer, but she wasn't tall enough to reach. Rose was grateful that she didn't have to worry about Libby's small fingers getting caught in the wringer.

Hannah stayed away from the rollers. "Martha yelled at us not to touch."

"Martha's right. They can be dangerous."

They carried the basket out to the yard. Rose clipped each sheet to the line, tugged on the pulley, and clipped another while Libby and Hannah chased each other through the yard.

As Rose returned to this rhythm of Amish life, the knots in her soul had unraveled. She found a peace here that she'd never had in the city. In the city, her life moved at such a rapid pace, she barely had time to think. Here she worked harder physically, but everything moved more slowly. She found she missed the soothing repetition of daily life.

She'd done her best to maintain her core beliefs, and she'd never been comfortable in Englisch clothes. But her faith was more than outward appearance and avoiding technology. Those only set her apart from the world; they weren't the heart of her beliefs. Being here in her family home brought her back to the basics and reminded her of the important things in life—family, community, and God.

Hannah had let Libby catch her in their game of tag, and she fell on the ground, laughing. Libby joined her, and the two of them giggled together until Rose longed to join them. Days like this made her wish to return to Amish life.

In the late afternoon when it was time for milking, Rose gathered the children for the trek back to their house. Hannah skipped on ahead, finding her way through the fields without any direction from Rose. But Rose called her back when they reached the tree line, and they stayed together until they reached the farm. Once again, Hannah dashed ahead and into the barn.

"Daed," she yelled, "we washed sheets and cleaned the house and weeded the garden."

"That's good, Hannah." Jonathan's voice came from inside the house. He laughed as he came down the porch steps to join Rose. "I wonder how long it'll take her to realize she's talking to herself."

"Daed, where are you?" she called.

"I guess she figured it out."

Rose chuckled along with him. The tension of that morning seemed to have broken.

Jonathan opened the barn door. "I'm right here, Hannah."

Her face indignant, she stomped over to him. "I looked all over for you."

"Sometimes it pays to be patient and think before acting." Jonathan set a hand on her shoulder. "I worry that charging ahead may get you in big trouble sometime."

As they prepared the first cows for milking, a red light flashed on the desk in the small office at the back of the barn. Rose pointed to it. "What's that?"

Jonathan blushed. "The answering machine."

"You have a phone?"

"I need it for orders for the gardening business and to contact the milk trucks."

"I see." Rose smiled to herself to see him so ill at ease over something she'd come to consider a necessity. "Aren't you going to answer it?"

"I, um, usually don't until after milking. I try to limit my use, so I only check messages once, at the end of the workday."

Rose tried to imagine answering the phone only once a day. That would reduce stress. One thing she'd never gotten used to in New York was the constant ringing and buzzing of phones. People answered them in restaurants, grocery stores, doctors' offices, and even restrooms. They talked while they walked along the sidewalks and when they rode in taxis or buses.

"How do you know if it's an emergency?" she asked as she set Amos and Libby in the play area and gave them each a toy.

Jonathan shrugged. "They'll call back more than once."

He'd barely finished speaking when the phone rang. After it stopped, the message machine kicked on.

"Jonathan, Harve Becker here from Farm to Table Restaurant. I've left several messages. We got word that several food critics will be dining here this evening, and we'd like some of your freshest specialty vegetables if you can deliver them before five or so. Call me back so we know what we can include on the menu."

Jonathan hurried into the office. "Looks like he called six times.

Too bad it's at milking time. I picked some nice vegetables earlier today."

"Go ahead and go," Rose called after him. "Hannah and I can handle the milking while you're gone."

Jonathan stood in the doorway of the office. "That's too much to ask of you."

"I don't mind. Besides it's my last day. This way I can go back to the city and tell people I milked fifty dairy cows. Everyone will be impressed."

A strange look crossed Jonathan's face. "But you've never done it before."

"I've milked lots of cows, I've helped you the past few days, and I have Hannah here in case I need any expert advice."

Jonathan laughed. "If I leave now, I might make it there and back in time to help you finish up."

"Go call him. We'll be fine." Rose had already wiped down several cows' udders with disinfectant and attached the suction cups of the milking machine.

Jonathan rushed into the office and a few minutes later raced from the barn. "I'll hurry."

Rose wanted to have the milking done before he got back, so she kept moving along, and Hannah helped. She enjoyed the way they worked together. Rose was finishing the last cows when Hannah scampered off. She assumed Hannah had gone to join Libby and Amos.

A few minutes later, Hannah called out, "Rose, I'm going to throw down some hay."

Rose glanced up to see Hannah leaning out over the hayloft far overhead. A bale of hay hung partway over the edge, and Hannah was examining it to see why it appeared to be stuck.

"Get back!" Rose screamed, but Hannah ignored her.

The small girl got behind the bale and shoved her shoulder into it. "No, Hannah!" Rose dashed toward her as Hannah gave a mighty heave. The bale of hay plummeted over the edge to the ground, and so did Hannah.

18

"Hannah!" Rose screamed as she dashed to where the small girl had fallen. Blood pounded in her ears, and her stomach churned as she knelt beside Hannah's still body.

Her nursing skills kicked in, and she did a quick assessment. Hannah's breathing and vitals were normal, but she was unconscious, and her leg was twisted at an unnatural angle.

Rose grabbed her cell phone and called 911. Ordinarily, in emergencies she was calm and collected, but this was Hannah and she'd been babysitting. She'd failed in her responsibility, and she was frightened for the little girl.

She babbled into the phone about the fall and Hannah's vitals and her leg . . . Then she tripped up on the address. Besides being panicky, it had been years since she'd been here. She remembered the street but not the house number, so she babbled about the cross street and counted the houses.

"Just relax, honey. We have GPS. They'll find you."

All of it seemed to be taking too much time. "Please hurry," Rose added. "She's unconscious."

"They're on their way," the woman assured her.

Clutching her phone so hard her hand hurt, Rose called the restaurant to let Jonathan know. She hoped he hadn't made his delivery yet and that the person who answered the phone could make sense of her babbling. "Please tell him to go straight to the hospital."

"What hospital, ma'am? There are several in the city."

Once again, Rose had no idea. She named the hospital where her Daed had been taken, but what if she sent Jonathan to the wrong one?

Finally, she called the operator to get the number of the Englisch neighbor across the street from Martha. After all the times Martha had accused Rose of being careless and unfit to care for Jonathan's children, Rose had to swallow down her shame to ask the neighbor to send Martha to Jonathan's to come and get the children. They couldn't go in the ambulance with her. At least she didn't have to talk directly to Martha. At least not until Martha arrived here, and they met face-to-face.

"Hannah hurt her leg," Rose told the neighbor. "She'll be transported by ambulance, but someone needs to come to Jonathan's house to watch the two little ones."

"It'll be all right, honey. It's only her leg," the neighbor said. "I'll run right over and tell Martha. You just relax."

"Please make sure she brings some bottles and a diaper bag." Rose had noticed Jonathan was low on diapers when she packed the diaper bag to take to her house. She didn't know if there were any clean bottles.

By the time she finished the phone calls, her body was trembling and her hand had deep indentations from squeezing the phone tightly. This was one time she wished she wasn't a nurse. She could think of so many possibilities and complications.

She felt so helpless. All her training, and she could do nothing to help Hannah. All she could do was sit here, terrified, and wait.

No, she could do something else, something she should have done from the start. Taking a deep breath, she placed a hand over Hannah's and bowed her head.

The words tumbled out for Hannah's healing, for Jonathan, for the EMTs who were coming. For Martha and David. For the doctors who would treat Hannah. And then for herself. For calmness and wisdom, and most of all, forgiveness.

As she prayed, a sense of calm descended over her. It had been a long time since she'd talked to God like this, and Rose realized how important her faith was to her. Not just in emergencies, but knowing God was there and had been with her every step of the way, no matter how rebellious she'd been. Her faith and trust in God had always supported her, been a part of her, and she couldn't leave it behind, no matter how far she ran.

Tears trickled down her cheeks as she made her peace with God.

Jonathan sat in a traffic jam, fuming as the minutes ticked by. The restaurant wanted the delivery by five, and he wouldn't make it on time. The chefs would be frantic. Harve had been waiting for a big break for his new restaurant. This might be it. He'd raved about how important these critics were to his success, and now Jonathan might be causing him to substitute something else at the last minute.

Irritation wouldn't make the traffic move faster, so Jonathan turned to prayer. His parents had taught him that everything happened in God's timing and that whatever happened was God's will. If that was true, he was right where God wanted him to be right now. He didn't know why, but his part was to trust.

He prayed for Harve, for those caught in traffic around him, and then for his children, and for Rose. At times, she seemed to be a lost soul. He didn't understand her decision to leave the Amish, but he prayed that God would lead her where He wanted her to go, even if it meant to the Englisch world. It tore Jonathan apart to pray those words, but they felt right and true. He wanted the best for Rose.

The traffic inched slowly past a construction site, and drivers honked at Jonathan for not picking up speed after he went by. Several leaned out and yelled at him or cursed him, but Jonathan's sense of serenity stayed with him as they whipped around him, sending sprays of gravel clattering against the buggy.

Jonathan reached the restaurant almost a half hour late. He hoped Harve's chefs still had time to make their special dishes. After gathering his crates, he knocked on the service entrance door.

Harve himself opened it. "Thank heavens you're here." He nabbed the nearest kitchen helper and told him to rush the crates to the head chef.

Jonathan turned to go, but Harve grabbed his arm. "Hang on a minute." He stuck his head through the kitchen door and bellowed, "Jason!" Then he turned to Jonathan. "The kid has a message for you."

"Huh?" Jonathan had no idea what a kid from the kitchen would want.

Jason burst through the door. "You Jonathan? Listen, some lady called practically in hysterics. She said your kid was going to the hospital. Aw, shoot, I forget her name. Ann, maybe?"

"Hannah?" Jonathan tensed. "Did she say what was wrong?"

"Broken foot or leg or something?" The kid didn't look too certain.

How would Rose get Hannah to the hospital? And what about the other kids? How would Hannah get a broken foot? Did a cow step on it? Kick her? "Did she say anything else?"

"Nah, man, that was it. Like I said, she was broke up about it. Not sure she was thinking clearly."

That didn't sound like Rose. She always appeared so calm and in control. Besides, she was a nurse and used to dealing with emergencies.

Jonathan rushed to the door. "Wait," he called after Jason. "Did she say what hospital?"

Jason turned. "Oh, right. I did ask her that. She mumbled something about her Daed being in that hospital."

Jonathan didn't wait to hear the rest. He knew where they'd taken Rose's Daed. As he pulled the buggy out into rush-hour traffic, he railed against the slowness. How long would it take to get there at this speed? He should have asked Jason how long ago they took her. Had Rose called from home or the hospital?

And then he remembered. Here he was, fretting about when he'd arrive. Hadn't he just had a lesson in God's perfect timing? If he'd made it to the restaurant by five, he'd have missed Rose's call. He would have gone home and had to drive all the way back to the city in rush-hour traffic.

Thank you, Lord, for directing my path. Help me to trust Your timing rather than my own.

Rose had just finished praying when an ambulance siren sounded in the distance. The whirling grew louder, which meant it was coming in their direction. She didn't want the ambulance to scare Hannah if she woke, but it screamed into the driveway. Had she told the woman they were in the barn? She might have when she rambled about the hay and hayloft.

It stopped near the back of the house, and Rose stuck her head out of the barn and waved and yelled.

Libby clapped her hands over her ears and bawled. Amos joined her in howling. Rose hurried over to the play area and picked them both up. Balancing one on each hip, she turned away so they weren't facing Hannah as the EMTs rushed into the barn. Rose wanted to watch them, but she worried Libby might be upset to see what was happening to Hannah, so she took them outside. The noise was louder out there, so she headed toward the kitchen.

Before she reached the back door, David pulled the buggy past the ambulance and onto the grass so it was out of the way of the barn. He hadn't even pulled to a stop before Martha hopped out and raced toward Rose.

"Where's Hannah?" she demanded.

"In the barn, but the EMTs are working on her now."

"Working on her?" Martha screeched. "What does that mean? I thought you said she had a broken leg."

She reached for Libby and practically wrenched her out of Rose's arm. She turned to her husband and thrust the little girl at him. "Hold her while I get Amos." Then she took Amos, cuddling him close. "I don't want you touching any of these children again."

Rose squeezed her eyes shut to prevent the tears she'd been holding in from falling. She'd never hold any of Jonathan's children again because she was leaving tomorrow. Her last day for making memories had turned into a nightmare.

"What hospital are they taking Hannah to?" Martha demanded.

"I'll find out." Rose hurried over to the ambulance and asked the driver. She was relieved to find out she'd directed Jonathan to the correct one—if he'd gotten the message.

She told Martha, who relayed it to David. "We should leave now because it'll take us much longer to get there," Martha said, and David nodded. "Someone needs to be at the hospital for Hannah. Does Jonathan know?"

Rose explained she'd left a message but didn't know if he'd received it. She was relieved when Martha and David left. Martha had spent the whole time shooting eye daggers at Rose. With no children to occupy her, Rose stood wringing her hands and watching the barn door. What was taking so long? Were Hannah's injuries more extensive than she thought?

Calm down, Rose. A small, quiet voice in her head reminded her to stop worrying and start praying. Again, that sense of tranquility came over her. A sense that all was well and under God's control.

Rose had finished another round of prayers for everyone when the barn door banged open and the EMTs pushed Hannah to the ambulance. Although she might not be welcome at the hospital, Rose wanted to ride along. She had to find out the extent of Hannah's injuries, and she prayed they weren't serious. Although she wanted to ride in the back, they sent her up front. Once again, in the space of less than a week, she was in an ambulance. Had God been providing opportunities for her to be around the medical field to remind her of her profession?

As they zoomed toward the city, Rose hoped Jonathan had gotten her message and had headed for the hospital. All she wanted to do was be encircled by his arms, but she'd been careless in watching his daughter. Would he be as angry with her as Martha and David? Would he even speak to her?

19

Jonathan arrived at the hospital and pulled his wagon into the same place he'd used before. He tied the horse to one of the hitching posts and jogged to the emergency entrance. If Hannah was coming in an ambulance, that was where they'd bring her.

As he rushed through the door, he flashed back to the last time he was here with Rose. She'd been sitting in the far corner. That's where she was this time too. The minute she spotted him, she came running over.

"I'm so sorry, Jonathan. I should have been paying closer attention."

Her teary eyes made him want to wrap his arms around her and hold her close. "What happened? They said something about her foot or leg?"

"Her leg is broken. I think they need you to sign some papers at the desk." Rose accompanied him to the counter, and they waited in line. "I was finishing the last cows when Hannah called out that she was throwing down some hay."

Jonathan sucked in a breath. "She climbed up to the hayloft?" He pictured his little daughter that high off the ground. "She knows she's never supposed to climb up there."

"I wish I'd been watching her." Rose's voice shook. "She'd pushed a bale of hay partway over the edge. I yelled for her to stop, but she pushed hard and—" Rose covered her face with her hands.

"Oh, Rose." Jonathan encircled her with his arms.

She lifted her head. Her eyes were filled with terror, as if she were reliving the scene. "I ran toward her, but I was too late."

They'd reached the window, and Jonathan signed some paperwork. Then the woman behind the counter pointed down a hallway. "They're ready to take her into surgery."

"Surgery?" Jonathan felt as if someone had just clobbered him over the head. His little girl in surgery?

Rose's voice was barely a whisper. "Her leg was twisted at an odd angle, and she was unconscious."

"Why didn't you tell me?" Jonathan demanded as the next person in line pushed past them.

"I didn't want you to worry. I was afraid you might rush to get here and have an accident, and I didn't want anything to happen to you."

Jonathan shook his head back and forth, trying to rid himself of the image of Hannah broken and unconscious on the barn floor with Rose leaning over her.

"I'm sorry. So, so sorry," she said.

Swallowing hard, Jonathan wrapped his arm around Rose's shoulder as they headed down the hall.

"Jonathan!" Martha's shrill voice echoed down the hallway. Carrying Amos, she came rushing after him. David trailed behind her carrying Libby.

Jonathan and Rose turned to face them. At the look of distaste on Martha's face, Rose shook off his arm and shrank back in shame.

Martha glared at Rose and then directed her attention to him. "I told you she couldn't be trusted."

All four of them headed to the surgical waiting room. Jonathan wished he could comfort Rose, but she backed away under Martha's scrutiny. He also tried to cut off Martha's criticisms of Rose, but she continued to blame Rose for Hannah's accident.

Martha's mouth finally snapped shut when the doctor entered to talk to Jonathan. Although he wished Rose would come along, she stayed where she was, while Martha and David crossed the room with him.

His face grave, the doctor explained that Hannah's leg required three pins, and she had a concussion. "According to the EMTs, she was unconscious when they arrived, but—"

"Unconscious?" Martha gasped and glowered over her shoulder at Rose.

Rose sank lower in her chair and looked distressed.

"As I was saying, although she was unconscious, she came to in the ambulance and responded to questions. Evidently, she also quizzed them."

Jonathan hid a smile. That was Hannah. If she'd been awake enough to question the EMTs, then she must be all right. *Thank you, Lord.*

"We sedated her for surgery, so she's in recovery now. She'll be in her room in about an hour."

After the doctor left, Jonathan went to tell Rose the news.

"Oh, I'm so glad she woke in the ambulance. I worried about her." Rose smiled. "I can picture her questioning the EMTs."

"So can I." Jonathan chuckled. "I'm guessing that means she's not going to have any lasting effects from that fall, once her leg's healed."

Rose hoped not, but it didn't lessen her guilt. And Martha added to it each time she looked at Rose.

"We're going to take Libby and Amos to the cafeteria for something to eat. Are you ready?" Jonathan asked.

Rose had no intention of spending the next hour or so under Martha's resentful glares, so she declined. "I'd like to check on my Daed, but afterward I'll stop by to see how Hannah is."

Jonathan's eyebrows rose. "Your Daed?"

"I'd like to try one more time before I go home. I'll check with Mamm and AnaMary first."

"I hope it goes well. I'll be praying."

"Thank you." Rose stood and accompanied them to the elevators. She got off on the second floor, relieved to escape from Martha's fury. They continued to the third floor to find Hannah's room before they went to the cafeteria.

When the elevator doors opened, Rose almost stayed inside. Remembering Daed's face before he collapsed and hearing his words made her reluctant to get off. Yet since she'd spent time taking care of Jonathan's children, she'd become more aware of the many ways Daed had cared for them as children. He'd taught her to milk cows, care for the horses, and do chores. She'd spent so much time resenting his criticism, she failed to realize how much work he'd done with no sons to help him. Many responsibilities fell to him, and he never once complained about all the work he had to do. He did it day after day with no expectation of thanks.

She should at least apologize for her rebellious attitude. After her prayer time earlier, Rose had been thinking about making an outward commitment to show her inner change. But joining the church meant taking baptismal classes. She couldn't stay here for the eighteen weeks that took. She needed her job to support herself.

She bowed her head. *Dear Lord, if this is Your will for me, please open a way for me to come back to the faith.*

Praying gave her the courage to walk down the hall to her father's room, but outside the door, she hesitated. She needed to consider his feelings. What if he didn't want to see her? What if she caused him to have another heart attack?

She'd hurt so many people she cared about. Maybe she'd be better off slipping away, going back home for the night, and calling a taxi in the morning to take her to the train station.

Uncertain about what to do, she bowed her head and asked for God's guidance and direction. When she lifted her head, it was with the certainty she needed to stay to make things right with others. She couldn't leave without asking for forgiveness from everyone—her parents, AnaMary, Jonathan, and Hannah. Even Martha.

A hand touched her shoulder, and Rose jumped. The old fear inside made her whirl around, and she found herself face-to-face with AnaMary. She let out her breath in a sigh and tried to relax the nerves that were making her edgy. She managed a smile.

"How's Daed doing?" she asked her sister.

"Why don't you come in and see for yourself?" AnaMary took Rose's hand and tugged her toward the door.

"I don't think that's a good idea. Last time he saw me . . . well, you know what happened."

"He's been different. The doctors and nurses have warned him about his temper. He doesn't always remember, but he's been trying hard."

"Seeing me might cause him to forget."

"Please, Rose?"

Rose whispered a quick prayer and entered the room with her sister. Across the room, Mamm sat in a chair next to the hospital bed, looking exhausted. Rose couldn't even imagine how hard it must be to sleep in that chair every night, especially with her arthritis. Seeing Rose in the doorway, she sucked in a breath.

Daed looked up. "Rose?" A pained expression crossed his face.

Fearful he'd kick her out before she had a chance to make things right, Rose plunged into her apology at the same time as her Daed spoke. They talked over each other before they both stopped midsentence. Rose dipped her head and motioned for her father to talk first.

Daed cleared his throat and glanced off into the distance for a moment. "Rose, several of the doctors and nurses told me you were responsible for saving my life. That without your quick action, I would have died."

Rose dismissed that with a wave of her hand. "It's what I've been trained to do."

Her Daed continued as if she hadn't spoken. "I understand it's no small thing, what you did. AnaMary described how you kept up with the CPR until the ambulance arrived. If you hadn't, I wouldn't be here."

Again, Rose brushed off her efforts. She'd done CPR on strangers, but for her own family, she'd do it as long as it took. "I'm glad it worked."

"Yes, well . . ." He lowered his eyes, and his hand clutched the edge of the blanket. "I, um, thank you, especially after"—his Adam's apple bobbed up and down—"after I was . . . unkind."

Unkind was a rather mild description for kicking her out, but this was her Daed. For him that was a huge concession.

Mamm moved to stand by the bed. She gave his shoulder a gentle squeeze as if encouraging him to go on.

He took a shaky breath and said the words the church had taught them to say. Words she'd been trained to say from childhood whenever she hurt someone. Words she'd never thought she'd hear from Daed. "Will you, um, forgive me?"

Rose was so stunned, she couldn't answer at first. Her eyes filled with tears, and she could barely nod. "Of course, I forgive you. But I came to apologize to you." She talked about realizing how hard it must have been for him to raise them and thanked him for all the things he'd done for them while they were growing up. "I never appreciated it when I was younger, but I do now. Most of all, I wanted to ask your forgiveness, especially for my rebellious attitude and for running away."

Daed's eyes had moisture in them as he said, "I forgive you, daughter."

Beside him, Mamm had tears rolling down her cheeks.

Rose's eyes were wet with tears as AnaMary hugged her. "I've missed you," AnaMary said. "I'm so glad you came back to visit, but it'll be hard to see you go."

Earlier she had been convinced she should join the church, but now she wondered if that was the right decision. A small nudge inside caused her to say, "I've decided I'd like to start baptismal classes." She'd take the first step and trust God's leading.

"Oh, Rose," Mamm said, her eyes shining. "I can't tell you how happy that makes us."

"But will you give up your New York job? Where will you stay?" AnaMary asked.

Mamm looked at Daed, a question in her eyes.

"If you need a place to stay," Daed said, his voice husky, "you could come home."

"Thank you, Daed." Rose felt as if she were coming home in more ways than one. Back to her home and family. Back to her church and faith. And back to God.

20

Hannah should be out of recovery by now. Rose asked at the desk and headed to the room number they gave her, but she stopped outside the door.

Martha's voice penetrated the door. "I warned you, Jonathan, about letting Rose near the children."

Rose cringed. She'd proved Martha right. She couldn't walk into that room to face Martha's rage. She wanted to apologize to Jonathan again for not watching Hannah more closely, but she couldn't do it in front of Martha.

Rose was about to slip away when David said, "She ruined Martha's life. I can't understand how you could possibly take a chance with your children after what happened to Martha. That should be proof enough about how irresponsible Rose is."

"What about what she did to her family? And to David?" Martha's voice rose. "Leaving without a word?"

"She was young back then, and you're right, she probably didn't think of the consequences. She's changed a lot. You should give her a chance. You should have seen her when Eli collapsed with the heart attack. She saved his life."

"Well, she ruined mine," Martha snapped. "And her carelessness could have cost Hannah's life."

Martha's words held so much anger and bitterness, Rose's stomach clenched. How had she hurt Martha that badly that her friend still harbored a grudge after all these years?

Maybe it was foolish, but Rose intended to find out what lay at the root of Martha's resentment. After a quick prayer for courage, she marched into the room. "Martha, before I left town, we were best friends. What did I do?"

Martha gasped. "What did you do?" She turned the scarred side of her face toward Rose. "You mean this?"

"I-I don't understand." Was Martha blaming her for the skin graft?

"Maybe you don't like facing up to what you've done. Running away to avoid responsibility is a cowardly thing to do."

"Running away?"

"I defended you to everyone, insisted you couldn't have started the fire, but when we discovered you'd run away to the Englisch that night, I knew the truth."

Rose struggled to understand what Martha was saying. A fire the night she ran away?

"You left me alone in the building that night and never told me you were leaving. When the fire started in the kitchen, I rushed around back to be sure you'd gotten out safely."

Rose pressed a hand over her mouth. There'd been a fire in the kitchen of Zook's Fry Pies after she left?

"The only thing I remember before I plunged into that building to look for you was seeing your Daed's buggy pull in front of the building. He jumped out and stood there yelling, 'Rose! Rose!'"

Daed had worried she was inside? He had no idea she'd run away.

"A crowd had gathered, and they said no one had come out of the kitchen. The fire engines arrived and the firefighters tried to stop me, but I broke away and ran into the burning kitchen. To save you!" Martha pointed a shaky finger at Rose as anger radiated from her.

Rose took a step back. Martha had risked her life to save her. And had been burned in the process? No wonder she'd been so cold and distant.

David picked up the story. "Even after the roof collapsed and Martha was taken away in the ambulance, I sat there coughing and choking with an oxygen mask on, refusing to let them take me to the hospital until they found you. I stayed until nothing was left but ashes."

David squeezed his eyes shut as if he couldn't bear the scene in front of him. "The only sound I remember besides the roaring fire and screaming sirens is your Daed calling your name, growing hoarser and hoarser until only wisps of smoke curled up from the wreckage."

Poor Daed. He'd paid a dear price for her rebelliousness.

"I let them take me to the hospital when all hope was gone." David opened his eyes and looked not at her but straight through her, as if he could penetrate all the way to her heart—a cold, callous heart that destroyed others' lives.

Rose cringed under his condemnation. But his condemnation was no greater than the criticism she had for herself and her selfishness.

"I loved you back then, Rose." David reached for Martha's hand. "Or what passes for love at sixteen." His eyes sought Martha's, and the love shining in his eyes had a depth Rose had seen only in her dreams.

"When the firefighters didn't find you inside, we hoped you'd escaped the fire," Martha said. "You never returned home that night, so they combed through the wreckage, looking for signs of you. I never knew until later."

"But I did." David sat forward, his eyes boring into her again. "As soon as I got out of the hospital, I spent every waking hour watching the investigators searching for bone fragments or clues. The only other person who stayed at that site until they'd sifted every fragment was your Daed."

What pain her Daed—and David—had endured. Martha too. All because of her.

Martha's face twisted into lines of distress. "Insurance investigators spent weeks examining the evidence. Once they'd established where and how the fire started, we all believed you'd run away because you were guilty."

David cleared his throat. "Martha almost lost her life trying to rescue you from that burning building. If she hadn't been dragged to safety . . ."

Martha gazed over at him with admiration shining in her eyes. "You risked your life to save me."

David's cheeks reddened, and he waved a hand as if to dismiss his heroics. "You were the brave one. Enduring all that pain and the skin grafts." He shook his head. "Never once complaining."

"What about you?" Martha leaned over and took his hand. "Suffering from smoke inhalation because you came after me. And all the while, we were worrying about you." Martha pointed at Rose. "Wondering if you'd survived. If they'd missed any clues." Tears trickled down Martha's cheeks. "I prayed every day that somehow you'd escaped."

Jonathan spoke for the first time. "We all did. We hoped . . ." He choked up. "Several weeks later, your cousin came to visit. That's when we discovered you'd left."

They'd agonized all that time? Rose couldn't imagine the pain they'd gone through.

"They ruled the fire accidental," Jonathan said.

"But it wasn't an accident, was it, Rose?" Martha's tone dared Rose to defy the accusation. Her eyes pinned Rose with barbs of fury. Martha was convinced of Rose's guilt. "Do you know how angry and betrayed we all felt when we discovered you'd run away? After all that, you never even faced your guilt. Never acknowledged what you'd done to all of us."

No wonder Martha had called her cowardly. They all believed she'd known about the fire. She couldn't speak nor defend herself because she was guilty.

Her eyes blazing, Martha turned to David and Jonathan. "I told you she was irresponsible. You didn't believe me, but now there's more proof." She pointed to the bed where Hannah lay sleeping.

Jonathan looked sick. He shook his head.

"Martha, please," David said, but she turned back to Rose, a triumphant look in her eyes.

All the accusations Martha had flung at Rose swirled through her head. Her carelessness had caused a fire, destroyed a business, hurt the people she loved, and scarred Martha for life. And now her carelessness had resulted in Hannah's hip cast. No apology could erase what she'd done. Leaping to her feet, Rose raced from the room.

"Running away again, Rose?" Martha's taunt followed her down the hall.

Rose rushed toward the elevator. Her eyes and throat burned, but no tears fell to quench her shame.

Footsteps pounded behind her. She dodged a meal cart rattling down the hall and jogged toward the elevator. The woman in the nurses' station frowned as she hurried past. She'd just pushed the elevator button when a deep, soft voice whispered, "Rose."

A strong hand landed on her shoulder, and she flinched. The old terror knotted her stomach, but the hand, gentle and steady, moved her away from the elevators and turned her to face him. Rose kept her head bowed. She couldn't bear to look at him.

Jonathan reached out and put a finger under her chin, tilting it until she met his gaze. "Are you all right?"

Rose shook her head. She wasn't sure she'd ever be all right again.

21

Jonathan opened his arms, and without hesitation, Rose walked into them. The minute she leaned against his broad, strong chest, the tears she'd restrained leaked out, dampening his shirt. He mumbled soothing words the way he did to Hannah when she wailed. The idea that Jonathan saw her as immature as his daughter made Rose weep.

When her tears were spent, she stayed still and silent, letting her head rise and fall with each breath he took, and under it all, she was comforted by the rapid staccato of his heartbeat. His strong arms stayed wrapped around her, protecting her, supporting her.

She didn't want to defend herself, but she wanted someone to know the truth. She lifted her head, and his eyes reflected no judgment, only empathy and understanding.

"I never knew." More tears overflowed as she said, "I had no idea about the fire."

The tilt of his head encouraged her to continue. Rose gave her account of that night. "I'd made arrangements to meet a car, so I cleaned up ten minutes early and left a note for Martha. I"—Rose clutched at her throat with one hand as if it could unblock the tightness—"thought I turned the fryer off. I-I must have turned it up instead of down."

"Oh, Rose." Jonathan's eyes reflected her distress.

She ducked her head, too ashamed to meet Jonathan's eyes. "When I glanced at the clock and saw I was going to be late, I tossed the dish towel toward the counter. I didn't look to see where it had landed. It must have landed in or near the fryer. I didn't mean to start a fire. I never would have left if I'd known."

Jonathan's expression showed he believed her. She longed to tell the others, but Martha would want no excuses, no justifications.

Rose had never told this story to anyone else, but the words tumbled out—from her fear in the phone shanty to meeting the car. "I made it as the car was pulling away. They stopped for me, and I got in. I was trembling from head to toe and wished I could jump out, but the car picked up speed and whisked me away. Away from the familiar landscape, away from everything I knew. We flew along so fast on the dark road, I grew dizzy. When we stopped, I had no idea where we were or how to get home."

Jonathan's arm tightened around her and gave Rose the courage to go on. "Looking back, that was one of the scariest nights of my life." All fear of her Daed's wrath paled in comparison. "I was surrounded by strangers. They gave me Englisch clothes to wear and a bed to sleep in. I'd never slept away from home before, and I was in a room with a few other runaways."

The worried look in Jonathan's eyes revealed his concern.

"I knew then I'd made a mistake, but I couldn't go back. I could only go forward, so I set my goal of being a nurse, and I achieved it." It had been a long, hard road, but—Hochmut or not—she was proud of what she'd accomplished.

Jonathan spoke for the first time since he'd taken her in his arms. "It sounds like you regretted leaving, so why have you chosen not to return?"

Rose couldn't, wouldn't give the real answer to his question. "I got used to New York and I love my job." That partial answer would have to suffice.

"But why did you run away in the first place?" Jonathan asked.

"Your Daed?"

"That wasn't the only reason." She didn't want to look him in the eye, so she lowered her head. "I-I fell in love with . . . someone I shouldn't have."

"I thought you were in love with David."

"No, he was in love with me." She made the mistake of glancing up and couldn't look away.

Jonathan's brow furrowed. "But the two of you were together all the time."

"Yes," she said miserably. "Only because the man I loved was courting someone else. I couldn't bear to see him marry someone else." As soon as she said it, she wished she could retract her words. Jonathan might realize she meant him.

What? Jonathan was sure he'd misheard. She'd loved someone other than David. It hurt him to think of her in love with anyone, but he understood the pain of unrequited love. How long had he been in love with her?

He had no business holding her like this. Yet with her softness pressed against his chest, her sighing breaths, her . . . How could he step away from her?

He kept his arms around her to be certain she wouldn't collapse. But his conscience jabbed him. He might be pretending he was doing it solely for her benefit, but the truth was, he never wanted to let her go.

He concentrated on the world around them—the dinging of the elevator, the clanging of the food cart, the phone ringing in the nurses' station. Anything to take his mind off what she'd said. Rose was Englisch now. For one wild minute, he entertained the thought of becoming Englisch so they could stay together, but he could never give up his faith. Never.

She'd made a fool of herself. Rose wished she'd kept that secret to herself. As soon as she told him, he couldn't get away from her fast enough. His arms had gone rigid, and he'd stepped back as soon as he made sure she could stand on her shaky legs without support.

Rose's cheeks burned. *Why did I confess my carefully guarded secret?* Secrets were meant to be private. She'd mistaken his pity for a deeper connection, and now she could barely look at him. Her fantasies that he'd been falling for her were dashed.

No matter what he thought of her, she'd come to apologize for her part in Hannah's accident and to offer her help. Rose forced out the words. "Jonathan, I'm so sorry about what happened to Hannah. I feel like it's all my fault. I—"

"Oh, Rose, no. Please don't blame yourself. We both know that Hannah's a handful. A lovable handful, but when she makes up her mind to do something, there's no stopping her."

"Like me." Those words perfectly described Rose too.

Jonathan chuckled. "I suppose that's true."

"Good that we both agree on that, because I've made up my mind to do something, and I won't let anyone stop me."

"I thought you'd already done that with your nursing."

"That was only the first step in the process. I plan to use that nursing experience in this new job of taking care of Hannah."

Jonathan stared at her, confusion on his face. "You're not taking Hannah to New York."

"Hmm . . . I bet she'd like that." Rose tried for a devilish glint in her eyes when she glanced at him sideways. "And you promised to ride on the subway."

"New York is out of the question. Not while Hannah's in a cast."

"Afterward then." Rose remained adamant, but she still hadn't told him what she had in mind. "I meant I wanted to prove to you how responsible I am and make up for my part in the accident by caring for Hannah at your house. I'm a trained nurse. I know everything that needs to be done during her recovery."

"This isn't making any sense. I'll be taking you to the train station tomorrow."

Rose gave him a teasing grin. "Oh, I forgot to cancel that ride. I received an invitation I couldn't pass up. Daed said I could move back home."

Jonathan leaned back against the wall, looking dazed. "I'm starting to think they sedated me instead of Hannah. Maybe you'd better start at the beginning so I understand."

Rose wasn't sure where the beginning was so she plunged in and told the story about visiting her Daed and how they both asked for forgiveness and how he offered to let her stay at the house and how she had decided to come home and how she planned to join the church. "And that's how I ended up deciding it would make sense for me to take care of Hannah."

Holding a hand in the air, Jonathan said, "I'm still feeling a bit lost, but you mean you're staying in Amish country for good?"

"That's the plan."

Jonathan appeared less than thrilled. "I see."

"You don't look very happy." Rose's words were tinged with hurt.

"Of course I am. It's just I'm still trying to take it all in. You moving back here and all. I also appreciate your offer to nurse Hannah."

"But—?"

"Well, there's Martha."

Martha. Rose had forgotten about her. "Do you think she'd accept my apology?"

Jonathan reached for her hand. "You need to tell David and Martha what you told me." He led her back to Hannah's room. "Rose has come back to stay. She listened to our side of the story. Now it's time to listen to hers."

At his urging, Rose told her version of the events. As she spoke, the haughty expression on Martha's face gradually softened.

When she finished, Rose hung her head. Ever since she'd arrived, she'd doubted Martha's friendship, thought her cold and unkind, when all along her friend had been harboring this hurt and grief.

Now Martha's nastiness made sense. "I never meant to hurt you." Rose broke down in tears. "Oh, Martha, I'm so sorry. Can you ever forgive me?"

Martha didn't answer. She just sat there, biting her lip and staring at the floor.

Rose walked over to where Martha was sitting and knelt on the floor in front of her. She put a hand up to touch Martha's scarred cheek. Martha jerked back as if stung.

Her throat clogged with tears, Rose said, "I know this is my fault, and I'm so sorry. I'd give anything for this not to have happened, but when you said it was because you'd gone in to search for me, I thought this was the most beautiful part of anyone's face I'd ever seen. It's pure love."

David came and stood beside Martha. "Every time I look at this side of your face, I see courage and caring. Rose is right. It is the most beautiful part of you."

Martha looked up at him with disbelief. The love shining in David's eyes when he met Martha's gaze made Rose long to have someone look at her that way.

22

Hannah's eyelids fluttered several times. Then she glanced around with half-closed eyes. "Daed?" she slurred. "Where am I?"

Relief swept over Jonathan. His little girl was awake and talking. She'd be all right. "In the hospital, Hannah."

"Why?" While he was still explaining about her fall, her eyes closed. "I'm tired."

Jonathan pulled a chair close to her bedside and took her hand. He closed his eyes too and rubbed his forehead with his other hand. Emotionally, he was drained after hearing Rose's story. And taking care of three children alone . . . Well, he had Martha and David's help and support, but ultimately, the full responsibility rested with him.

"Is there anything I can do?" Rose's soft words fell like a soothing balm on his ears. "I can do the milking tomorrow if you want to stay with Hannah."

Jonathan glanced up at her and then wished he hadn't. Her eyes still damp with tears and her tender expression made her a dangerous distraction. That old pull of attraction sucked the breath from his lungs. He could barely manage a thank-you.

Martha stood. "We should get these little ones home to bed." She turned a piercing gaze on Rose. Evidently, the apology hadn't cleared away all the animosity between the two of them.

Jonathan had some concerns about his children staying with Martha again, but he couldn't be in two places at once.

Martha hustled out the door with the children as if afraid he'd change his mind.

Rose stood too. She went to the opposite side of the bed and brushed a few loose strands of hair back from Hannah's forehead. "I'm so sorry."

"You've said that several times already," Jonathan said. "It was an accident, so there's no need to apologize."

"Maybe if I'd been watching more closely . . ."

"Milking cows takes a lot of concentration. It's hard to do that and watch children too. I should know." He wished he could erase the guilty expression from her face.

Rose nodded, but he could tell from her face she didn't believe it. "I should go. Did you want me to take your buggy back and feed the horse if you're staying for the night? I still need to feed the horses and chickens at your place and ours. I could bring the buggy back whenever you want it. That is, if you trust me to drive it."

His whole body caught fire when he remembered teaching her. He tamped down the feelings overwhelming him and tried to sound neutral and encouraging. "You did fine with it. I'm sure you can get it home. Just be careful in traffic."

When Rose left, he wished he could go with her to see how she did. Not that he didn't trust her. He did. He only wanted to be on the seat beside her, dreaming of holding her. Or perhaps making an excuse to correct some minor mistake so he'd have an excuse to touch her.

Rose missed Jonathan's presence as she did the chores both at his place and at home. Over the next few days, she fit right into the day-to-day rhythm of Amish life—the early risings, the daily chores, the hard work, the early bedtimes—but other adjustments weren't as easy. She still reached for light switches whenever she entered a room, and she missed doing her laundry in electric washers and dryers instead of the wringer washer and clothesline. Some nights she longed for a dishwasher and microwave, and she struggled to get used to a battery-powered lamp for lighting her way to bed.

When Daed was discharged, she cooked special meals for him, and gradually, the two of them worked on their relationship. The tension between them decreased after Rose spoke with the bishop about attending baptismal classes. She was nervous about the decision, but after talking with Bishop Troyer and praying about her decision, a deep sense of peace came over her and she knew she'd made the right choice.

Giving up her furnished New York apartment, telling her roommates to divide up or sell her things, and saying goodbye to everyone she'd worked with was heart-wrenching, but Rose remained steadfast in her choice when they tried to persuade her to return to city life. Some of her friends teased her and said she wouldn't last in the old-fashioned life and would soon be back, but Rose ended the conversations knowing she'd found her true home with her community, her family, and God.

On the day Hannah was discharged, Rose drove the buggy to the hospital to get her and Jonathan. On the way back, she let Jonathan drive, which gave her the opportunity to sneak peeks at him. She also turned around to talk to Hannah in the back seat.

As they pulled into the driveway, Rose offered again to care for Hannah.

"I can't ask you to do that," Jonathan protested. "You've done so much for us already."

"I'd like to do it. I miss nursing and . . ." She turned pleading eyes to him. "It would ease my conscience."

"Rose, you have nothing to feel guilty about."

"Please, Jonathan?"

"Please, Daed," Hannah said. "I want Rose to be my nurse."

He set down the reins and pretended to throw his hands in the air. "What can I do with both of you begging me?"

Hannah cheered loudly, a sentiment Rose's heart echoed. She looked forward to spending more time with the little girl and, of course, her Daed.

For the next few weeks, Rose enjoyed taking care of Hannah. At first the little girl chafed at being confined to bed and to a cast, but soon she was devising ways to do daring things despite her cast. Rose spent quite a bit of time chasing her and finding games or chores to keep her occupied. Jonathan cut down a walker from a secondhand shop to her size, and soon Hannah was playing tag and helping with the milking.

Libby and Amos had become attached to Rose, which bothered Martha. But a short while after Hannah came home from the hospital, Martha started spending her mornings in bed, feeling ill. Rose suspected there would be a new baby in the household, but Martha only looked at her sadly when Rose mentioned it.

"I can't get my hopes up." Martha stared off into the distance. "I've lost five already."

As the months went on, she grew more confident, and she and Rose began planning for the new little one. Sewing baby clothes, making quilts, and helping Martha paint the room for the baby filled Rose with joy.

As Rose was leaving after assisting with the room, Martha stopped her. "Thank you for your help. I . . . um . . . there's something I need to say." She avoided Rose's eyes and plucked at her black work apron with nervous fingers. "I owe you an apology for how I treated you when you first arrived. You've been so kind, and I regret harboring all that anger toward you."

Rose reached for Martha's hands, but her friend drew them back and tucked them in the folds of her apron.

Then Martha's cheeks colored. "I'm sorry," she mumbled and extended her hands.

Rose took them in both of hers. "After you've forgiven me for all I did, I certainly forgive you."

"You haven't heard everything yet." Martha stared down at the floor. "I've been jealous of you since we were teens. The only boy I ever loved spent all his time with you."

"David? But you never wanted him around . . ." Rose trailed off at the pain on Martha's face. Now she understood. Martha hadn't wanted him around Rose. How could she have been so blind? "I wish I'd known."

"It wouldn't have made a difference. David had eyes only for you. The way you had eyes only for Jonathan."

Rose drew in a sharp breath. "You knew?"

"It was plain to me why we spent so much time at their house."

Had Jonathan known too? She'd hinted at the truth that night in the hospital. He must have figured it out, or maybe he'd known all along, the way Martha had. Was that why he'd been keeping his distance and avoiding her? Rose cringed. She'd made a fool of herself.

Martha, her voice thick with tears, continued, "David never would have looked at me if it weren't for the fire. I still think he married me out of pity. He says not, but I've always wondered." She swallowed hard and choked out, "When you came to the door that night, all I could think of was that I'd lose him."

"But you're married."

"I know." Teardrops sparkled on Martha's eyelashes. "David would never do anything dishonorable, but what if in his heart, he wished he'd married you instead of me?"

"Oh, Martha." Rose reached out and pulled her friend into an embrace. "When we were at the hospital with Hannah, I was so jealous when David looked at you with such love. Not that I want David, but I only hope and pray a man looks at me that way someday." *Not just any man, though. Only one will do.*

"Really?" Martha pulled back to look Rose in the eye.

Rose nodded. "Yes, really."

Martha squeezed her eyes shut. "I've carried this burden for years, and it's eaten away at my soul. Will you forgive me?"

Her throat too tight to speak, Rose could only nod, but her heart overflowed with gratitude to God for restoring their relationship.

Now if she could only find a way to bridge the uneasiness with Jonathan. She might never have his love, but she'd at least like to be friendly, to talk and share, to have fun together.

Jonathan touched the leaves of his budding plants, tenderly and gently, the way he wished he could caress Rose's face. Something he'd never be able to do. If only he hadn't seen her face when she told him she'd been in love with someone else all those years ago. Her eyes showed she still cherished that long-ago love. He tried to remember the boys in her buddy bunch and guess who had won her undying love.

Each time she brushed past him or he looked up and met her eyes, that past love stood between them, haunting him. When he watched her tenderness with Hannah or saw her cuddling Amos and Libby, he wanted to reach out and fold her in his arms. Instead he responded gruffly to cover his longing.

Working together every day, often eating meals together, coming into the kitchen and seeing her at the stove ripped him apart inside. He wanted her so badly, but he needed to respect the mourning period and Rose's feelings for another. After the mourning period ended, he struggled even more with the temptation to hold her. Only the memory of that burning passion in her eyes kept him from acting on his impulses.

Then one day it occurred to him Rose's true love likely had married another, the way he'd married Esther to forget Rose. Over time, he'd grown to love Esther. Perhaps Rose could come to care for him. She already loved his children, and the two of them worked well together. He loved her and would take good care of her. He could at least mention the possibility of making their partnership permanent. Several men at church, some widowers like himself, some much older, appeared to be considering her. It might be best to ask her before they had a chance.

Once he'd made the decision, his spirits lifted, only to come crashing down. Suppose she rejected him? Could they go back to working together, spending time together, having fun together? What if he ruined their friendship?

Rose had made peace with God as well as with Daed and Martha. Helping Mamm and AnaMary with the chores and cooking brought them closer together. Gradually, they relaxed with each other, and soon the kitchen was filled with teasing and laughter. Rose felt like she'd come home at last.

The only area of her life that made her sad was her relationship with Jonathan. He was friendly and polite, and they worked together as a team, but he was often distant. The only time he grew animated was when he taught her about growing specialty vegetables. She cherished their time together. The aisles were so close they brushed past each other. Each time they did, Rose's pulse fluttered. She worried her sharp intakes of breath would give away her true feelings.

She tried to console herself that Jonathan was still in his mourning period, but when that ended and he seemed to avoid her even more, she grew despondent. Perhaps he wasn't God's will for her. Rose prayed that God would show her what He wanted her to do in the future. She'd loved Jonathan for so long, it was hard for her to think she could possibly marry someone else.

One afternoon Jonathan surprised her. "It's a lovely day. I thought we could see if Martha would babysit, and we could take a picnic lunch to the quarry."

"That sounds like fun." Rose hoped maybe this would be the start of their courtship.

But when she got into the buggy, Jonathan acted morose or . . . or . . . Rose couldn't quite figure out his odd mood, but it seemed as if he didn't want to be around her. His stiffness made her edgy, and she wished she'd stayed back at the house with the children. She would have had more fun. Even cajoling him to talk about his beloved vegetables didn't pull him out of his shell. The rest of the ride was spent in uncomfortable silence.

Jonathan had planned to have the picnic first and then ask her, but his stomach was so knotted up, he needed to get his question out of the way first. He took a deep breath to calm his frazzled nerves. "Rose, that night in the hospital, you mentioned being in love with someone."

Her cheeks matched the cherries he'd packed in the picnic basket, and she lowered her eyes. "I was hoping you'd forgotten that."

How could he ever forget hearing she loved someone else?

"I didn't want you to know," she said, her words barely above a whisper. "But if Martha figured out why we were at your house all the time, I guess you did too."

Their house? She hadn't loved David. That meant—

"Rose, look at me."

When she did, her eyes revealed the truth. Jonathan struggled to control the emotions racing through him. Her words unleashed the torrent of feelings he'd hidden for years. If only he had known.

Rose trembled as he reached for her hand.

"I was in love with you back then." Jonathan's voice was husky. *He was?* "But Esther?"

He squeezed his eyes shut. "Everyone thought you and David . . ." He swallowed hard. "I courted Esther, hoping to forget you, but I never did."

If he never forgot her, did that mean he still loved her? "You-you loved me?"

"Yes, I loved you then. I still do. And I always will."

Everything she'd ever dreamed of and wanted. Her fingers entwined with his, she was so overwhelmed she couldn't speak. But there was no need to speak.

With birds twittering overhead and a soft breeze caressing their faces, he cupped her face in his hands and pressed his lips to hers, and her heart sang as she kissed him back with equal enthusiasm. And when he pulled away, the love shining in his eyes was everything she'd always dreamed of and more.

Up to this point, we've been doing all the writing. Now it's *your* turn!

Tell us what you think about this book, the characters, the plot, or anything else you'd like to share with us about this series. We can't wait to hear from *you*!

Log on to give us your feedback at:
https://www.surveymonkey.com/r/HeartsOfAmish